FIRE IN THE BLOOD

SHARDS OF A BROKEN SWORD: BOOK TWO

W.R. GINGELL

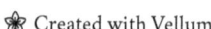

For my favourite little Sis. She corrects all my inconsistencies and finds all my missing words.

Sometimes she even does it for my books.

PRELUDE

By and large, slavery to Crown Prince Akish was actually quite boring. It was true, thought Rafiq, observing the prince from high overhead, that Prince Akish was vicious, overeager for a fight, and inclined to treat every life but his own with a careless abandon. In spite of that, he was the best swordsman the Kingdom of Illisr (and most likely the surrounding kingdoms) had ever seen, he had a serpent's cunning for his campaigns, and he very rarely called on Rafiq to assist him in any but his most dangerous ventures. Thus it was that Rafiq, after fifteen years of slavery, had only ever contributed to a handful of the Prince's more dangerous operations. He had been young when the prince's father captured him: young but already formidably strong, with his first battle scars beginning to whiten on him. And although in time he began to forget what it was like to be free, he never forgot that he *had* once been free. Prince Akish, while he didn't choose to enlist Rafiq's superior strength for most of his campaigns, liked to have Rafiq accompany him everywhere– a sign both of his power and his nobility.

And Rafiq, doing what dragons do best, allowed his anger to

simmer beneath the surface like dragonfire; molten, deadly, and ready to be called upon at the right time.

There was always a false kind of freedom to flying. Rafiq, wheeling left to keep Akish in sight and ease the burden of the incorporeal thread that bound him to the prince, bared his teeth to the wind. The prince had only tried to ride Rafiq once, when Rafiq's sudden desire to display his skill with barrel-rolls, needlessly sharp turns and sudden plunges for the ground had the prince simultaneously throwing up and tumbling to the grass in an undignified heap. That had ended the appalling humiliation of having a human rider, but it did make things unpleasant when it came to keeping in range of the prince. By dint of painful experimentation, he'd since discovered that the bond would allow him a distance of roughly three miles in any direction before it clawed at him to return. There was also the added advantage that if the prince forgot to attach his communication spell to Rafiq's ear, Rafiq wasn't able to hear any Commands. The spell that bound him to the prince only bound him to obey spoken Commands, and if Rafiq took to the air without the communications magic, he was able to fly in the constrained freedom of his three miles for as long as he chose while Prince Akish danced in helpless rage below. He paid for it afterward, of course, but every tiny rebellion was worth it.

"Come down, Rafiq," said the prince in his ear. "We're getting close."

Rafiq flipped lazily in the air and descended in a loose spiral. He glided close by the prince's horse, maliciously spooking the gelding, then met the ground with practised ease, his callused pads battering the grass flat and his claws tearing out chunks of turf as he went.

Prince Akish's nostrils were flaring when Rafiq loped back to him. "Heel, you son of a lizard!" he said through his teeth. Rafiq came to heel, the spikes of his wingblades slapping the horse's flanks and prompting further panic from the poor beast.

The prince viciously hauled on the reins but didn't repeat his insult. Those were the rules. If Prince Akish wasn't clear enough in his Commands, he was well aware of who he had to blame.

"Don't spook my horse," he said instead. "And prepare yourself: I have need of you."

-Am I polishing your armour or acting as a herald to your arrival?-

"Neither," said the prince. "There's a dragon I need you to kill."

Through a curl of smoke and flame, Rafiq said: *-What dragon? There are no dragons of note in Shinpo. Or is it a purge of the lesser beasts?-*

"No purge," Prince Akish said. There was a sharp smile on his face: bespeaking acquisition and not humour, if Rafiq wasn't mistaken. "But you're wrong about Shinpoan dragons of note. Even a lizard like you must have heard of the Enchanted Keep."

Rafiq let a delicate stream of fire purr against the setting sun. He'd seen the vague suggestion of a tower from his position in the air, but he'd never heard of the Enchanted Keep. It was possible that the prince and his cronies had mentioned it, but since Rafiq tried to block out their back-slapping and shouts of laughter whenever he could, it was also possible that he'd ignored that too.

Against Rafiq's silence, the prince said irritably: "The third Shinpoan princess was taken captive by the dragon of the Enchanted Keep five years ago. Her family already had their heir and their spare, so it wasn't advertised, but I've recently had reports that the family aren't as ruthless with their children as they'd like us to think. It could prove useful to have the girl as a bargaining chip. And if nothing comes of *that* it's always useful to rescue a princess. People like it."

Anyone who wasn't the princess or her unfortunate family, thought Rafiq. Prince Akish was already trying to oust his own father from the throne of Illisr: it didn't bear thinking about what he could do to the neighbouring Shinpo if he had a princess as hostage.

-That's all?- he said. *-We travelled to Shinpo to kill a single dragon?-*

"No, we came to kill an Enchanted Keep," said the prince. "It's said that the Keep has the dragon in thrall. Whether or not that's true, the dragon is only one challenge: there are seven circles of challenge to defeat before the princess can be rescued. She's in the highest room of the tallest tower, sleeping an enchanted sleep until her rescuer braves all seven circles and overcomes them."

Rafiq gave a fiery cough of laughter. How very human and complicated. *-What are the circles?-*

"No one knows," said the prince, with a satisfied smile. "No one has yet made it past the dragon."

THE FIRST CIRCLE

There was no dragon in sight when the prince and Rafiq cautiously approached the Enchanted Keep. Rafiq, bearing in mind the prince's information that the princess was kept captive in the highest room of the tallest tower, was sourly amused to see that the Keep only boasted one tower. It was built on a jagged outcrop of stone and dark green grass, rising white and slim against the blue sky from a white, paved courtyard; and it didn't seem big enough to obscure a dragon from their sight. Or, if it came to that, hide the approach of one.

Rafiq began to feel slightly uneasy. He could sense the magic of the Keep spreading through the surrounding air like heat shimmer, warping and changing everything it touched. The very air around the tower was thick with magic, the breaching of which was like plunging into a thick fog.

"You're Burdened," Prince Akish said, thickening the air still further.

Rafiq snarled at the added weight. -*What are your instructions?*-

"Kill the dragon. Preserve my life. Complete the First Circle of Challenge."

Short and sweet. Rafiq savoured a laughing curl of fire in his throat. Prince Akish had learned that it was safer to give Rafiq clear, simple commands without any other possible interpretation than the obvious one. In this case, the prince was being even more careful than usual.

Formally, he said: *-I hear and obey-* and took to the sky in a swirl of wing-spikes and grass blades.

The first few strokes of his wings were heavy and laborious, but once he was properly in the air there was a fresh, strong updraft that wouldn't have been out of place by the sea. That made him uneasy, too. None of the surrounding countryside had led him to expect strong breezes here. Still, it made his ascent much easier. As he rose, the tower of the Enchanted Keep kept pace with him, a slender cylindrical edifice in pale bricks that turned out to be both much higher than it seemed, and much larger than it seemed. The closer he got, the clearer it was to Rafiq that the tower was not in fact built of a pale sandstone brick, but massive slabs of white marble that sat gravely one upon the other. From a distance the marble had looked like regularly sized bricks: closer to, Rafiq could see that each of the marble slabs was at least as big as he was.

There was still no sign of the other dragon. Rafiq, bound to ensure Prince Akish's safety as well as slay the other dragon, kept to his lazy, spiralling ascent, his gaze alternating between the prince and the scenery. The courtyard of the Keep made a small square beneath him, drawing in the velvet green countryside around it until the grass seemed to pucker by the force with which it was pulled. Rafiq found himself thinking that perhaps this time, Crown Prince Akish had bitten off more than he could chew.

The roof of the tower was light blue and gently conical, shingled in circular layers. Rafiq was inclined to admire the scale-like structure of it until it seemed to untwine itself dizzyingly from the top of the tower, and it occurred to him that the roof was moving. Only it wasn't the roof, it was a dragon that had been coiled around the pale blue roof, now uncoiling itself.

No: *her*self. This lithe, blue and silver beauty sweeping her tail around the spire of the tower was a she-dragon. Rafiq thought that he hung in the air without moving, even to flap his wings; but the hot and steady thump in his ears was certainly his wings beating against the updraft as they held him aloft. He purred deep in his throat and arched his wings before he knew what he was doing, but—perhaps fortunately—the she-dragon didn't respond in kind. Instead, her underscales irradiated with a rippling tide of burnt orange, bespeaking caution, and a slight edging of magenta that said she was curious. The growing rise of orange through her scales bought Rafiq forcibly to mind of his Burden, and the fire in his belly seemed to turn to ice. He tried to pull away and circle back to Prince Akish but the Burden clawed tight into his soul and sent him headlong at the she-dragon; a blunt, battering pass that she avoided with consummate ease.

His own unwilling clumsiness brought Rafiq to the unpleasant realisation that whether or not he wanted to, he would be forced to murder an innocent she-dragon. The only question was whether he would allow the Burden to do it for him in slow, clumsy, battering strokes, or whether he would do it himself in the quickest, most painless way possible.

The she-dragon danced on the updraft across the tower roof, light and quick, her scales now utterly black. Rafiq, with bitterness in his heart, clipped his wings tight to his sides and dove for her. The she-dragon fought like a shard of quicksilver, sharp and fast. She was faster, but Rafiq was stronger and his reach was longer: he was certain that once they came to grips the battle would be done. The problem, he discovered, as he twisted once more out of reach of her claws, was *getting* to grips with her. She was in and out with her slender claws before he had the chance to meet and close with her, leaving thin tears on his underscales. Fortunately his underscales were tougher than most and her claws didn't penetrate deeply enough to do more than draw blood. The slight pulling discomfort was enough to distract him slightly, however, and having to watch out for the prince didn't help his concentration.

Rafiq pulled himself tighter, protecting his underside, and the she-dragon went for his wings instead. He rumbled a fiery laugh and twisted, slicing hard and fast with his wing-spikes. She dodged, but he saw the spurt of red from one of her wings and the way she staggered in the air, and dove after her immediately. This time she wasn't quick enough, and Rafiq, with a surge of mingled regret and exultation, closed with her at last. He bound her tail with his, her wings pinned to her sides by his claws, and with a clean slice of his wing-spikes he slit her throat from one side of her jaw to the other shoulder. Then he held her close, warming her last moments with the fire that burned high and hot along his underside, and carried her gently to the courtyard below, blood bubbling over her scales and his.

* * *

IN THE SMALLEST room of the Enchanted Keep a young woman in serving garb lay sleeping on a narrow cot. A scar, lit from within, spread on her neck from one ear to the other shoulder. As a dark, complicated shadow sank past the window her eyes flew open and she sat up, gasping.

"Oh no!" she said, scattering pillows in her haste to scramble from the bed. "Oh no, no, no!" She leapt for the door without stopping to find her shoes and sprinted down the hall, her bare feet slapping against cool marble. A shadow passed the window again as she ran, huge and rising fast; but she ignored it.

As she approached the grand stairs that swept down into the receiving hall, a booming gong sounded through the Keep. The girl took the stairs three at a time with the practised ease of one who has done so many times before, fairly flying across the red-marbled hall below until at last she was by the grand doors, her breath quick and short. There she took a moment to straighten her head-dress and neck-scarf, unwrapping it completely only to wrap it again more carefully around the new scar. At last she took a slow, careful breath in, released it just as carefully, and hauled open one of the massive front doors.

The First Circle is ended.

3

THE SECOND CIRCLE

*R*afiq flew high and sank again. It was no use trying to run, but the furious energy in him demanded to be spent, and it wasn't until he'd expended it that he returned to Prince Akish in the courtyard below.

The prince threw him an impatient look when he landed. "Are you finished sulking?"

Rafiq spat a molten piece of fire and said: -*Yes*-

"Good. I'll have need of you once I'm in the Keep."

-*I won't fit*-

"You're Burdened," said the prince. "Be a man."

Rafiq snarled an even bigger ball of fire but there was nothing he could do. Burdened he had been, and Burdened he was to Change. His wings dwindled and disappeared into his shoulder blades, sparking the faint sense of panic that changing to human always induced in him, and the courtyard around him seemed to spring up, growing at ridiculous speed. When it was done he found himself crouched on the flagstones, chilled and small, with one stupidly delicate human hand flat against marble where it made a brown blot against the white. Somehow, whether from familiarity with Prince Akish's physiognomy or because of his own dusky scales, Rafiq always found himself as a vaguely earth-coloured human when he changed. It made him fit in with the general Illisran population, and if he'd assumed anything so specific, Rafiq would have assumed that he would take on the lighter caramel skin tone of the Shinpoan people when Changing in Shinpo.

He climbed rather unsteadily to his feet, aware that Prince Akish was waiting by the Keep's massive front doors with impatient black eyes, his fingers tapping an irregular tattoo on the grand marble balustrade beside him. There was a similarly large and ornate bell pull within easy reach of the prince– not that he'd bestir himself to pull it, thought Rafiq, with an unfamiliar human grin tugging at the corners of his mouth.

He managed to climb the stairs on his second attempt, precariously off-balance by the loss of his two forward legs, and set a resounding gong bellowing on the other side of the doors by a vigorous pull at the bell-chain. Beside Rafiq, the prince straightened his chain-mail and adjusted his sword to a more convenient angle: preparing for either female welcome or male attack.

Someone must have been watching for them, because the ringing tone of the gong had scarcely faded when one of the heavy double-doors groaned inward, spilling bloody light on the red marbled floor of the Keep's grand hall. Rafiq saw bare feet first, one of them white-scarred in a line that vanished beneath a fluttering hem of light pink. It was a girl– a serving girl, if Prince Akish's: "You there! Where is the princess?" was to be trusted.

The serving girl gave them a Shinpoan bow with her bare arms outstretched gracefully, displaying the top of her beaded head-dress for a respectful moment. She drew herself upright again in a single, liquid movement, and said in careful Illisran: "Your mightinesses are well-come and apologies are offered."

"Never mind that," said the Prince, in impatient and effortlessly colloquial Shinpoan: "I don't want your apologies, I want the princess. Bring her to me."

"Well, that's what I was trying to apologise about," said the serving girl. Rafiq thought she looked relieved to be speaking her native tongue. "You can't get to the princess. You've passed one Circle of Challenge, but there are six more to go. In fact, as soon as you step across the threshold the second Circle will begin, so you *really* might like to think about it before you– oh..."

Her voice trailed away as Prince Akish said to Rafiq: "Remove her," and Rafiq seized her by the elbows, lifting her bodily out of the way. He'd always thought his human form was ridiculously small, but it occurred to him for the first time that it was only so in relation to his dragon self. The serving girl's head only came to his shoulder, and now that he came to think of it, Rafiq found that he could see over Prince Akish's head without rising on the pads of his feet.

"You'll refrain from getting in our way," said the prince, crossing the threshold in Rafiq's wake.

The serving girl, flicking a look from Prince Akish to Rafiq, said: "I'm sure you're right. There's a Door Out if you need it, your highnesses. Don't hesitate to call if you should require me: I'll be in the next room."

She left them in a flutter of pink silk, the long end of her neck-scarf wafting lightly behind her. To Rafiq, it seemed as though she was decidedly cross. That was intriguing, because he'd always found female humans particularly hard to read. The moods and features of the prince and other Illisran males he had come to read tolerably well, but he hadn't had much of an opportunity to study the female of the species.

"Leave the serving girl alone," said Prince Akish, following Rafiq's eyes. "We don't need her. The princess is said to be in the highest room of this accursed tower: we'll ascend the main stairs and find our way from there. Be alert. Take the lead."

They weren't styled as Commands, but Rafiq felt the burden settle on him nevertheless. He crossed the hall in swift steps, his eyes darting into the bloody shadows that flanked it. It was hard to tell exactly how big the hall was, though it was clear that it was vast: the smudging of shadows far away were akin to an old oil painting. In fact, it didn't seem as though the hall ended so much as became two dimensional. Rafiq felt his eyes slide away from the far end in discomfort and started up the stairs. His human legs were beginning to feel more able, and he took the stairs two at a time with one ear to the prince's footfalls behind him. The curving balustrade framed the hall below, cool white against red, and rounded into a smooth bowl at the upper landing, from whence the front doors could be seen in the same kind of flat reality as the distant hall below. Rafiq grunted at that, missing the familiar heat of fire in the back of his throat, and passed ahead of the prince into the grand room that led on from the landing.

It was paved in the same red marble as the hall below. Rafiq grimaced in distaste, but the expression froze on his face as his eyes met the grand staircase at the end of the chamber– no, hall! He took several swift steps into the room and turned in a slow circle, his chin oscillating up and down in his study of the hall.

"It's the same as the one below," said Prince Akish. "It's exactly the same as the hall below."

Rafiq, who had been systematically scanning the hall, said: "It *is* the hall below. We're back where we started."

The prince said flatly: "That's impossible."

"Yes," agreed Rafiq, but he saw the prince's eyes flickering wildly around the hall.

"Confusing, isn't it?" said the serving girl's voice. She was in the doorway of the next room: the same one that she had entered in the hall below.

"How did you get there?" demanded Prince Akish.

Rafiq managed to restrain himself from sighing, though one of his brows rose, and when he chanced to meet the serving girl's eyes she was looking distinctly amused.

"I was here all along," she said. "I told you: there are another six Circles of Challenge. This is the second. It's a circular paradigm of two rooms and a staircase from which there are no exits except the way forward and the Door Out."

"She must have sneaked up the staircase behind us," said Prince Akish stiffly to Rafiq.

"She didn't," said the serving girl. "But don't take my word for it. Climb the stairs again. I'll wait for you."

"Climb the stairs again," said Prince Akish to Rafiq.

Rafiq's instinct was to bare his teeth in a snarl but his human face didn't know how to make the right shapes, so he grimly ascended the stairs without speaking. Trust Akish to do anything he could do to avoid being made a fool of! This time he kept Prince Akish and the serving girl in sight as he climbed, guiding himself by the balustrade. As it curved out into the familiar bowl shape of the landing once again, Rafiq took one last look at the others and strode into the room. The serving girl and the prince stood there before him.

"Here we are again," said the serving girl pleasantly. Rafiq gazed at her silently, then wheeled back to the stairs behind him. When he leant over the balustrade of the landing, the serving girl's eyes were on him from her place in the hall below. She gave him an elegant half-shrug.

"Come back in," said Prince Akish curtly, and when Rafiq crossed the landing once again, he added: "Close the doors. The other staircase is harping upon my nerves."

Rafiq did so, glancing up at the double doors at the top of the grand stairs in *this* room. He couldn't see them properly, but through the spokes of the balustrade he thought he saw wooden panelling. The top doors were now also closed.

Prince Akish turned on the serving girl. "What is this sorcery?"

"Just what I told you," she said. "This is the second Circle. Unless you take the Door Out, these are the only two rooms you'll see until you find the way forward."

"Give me the room," said Prince Akish, after a frowning moment of thought. "I need quiet."

The serving girl looked indignant, but she didn't resist when Rafiq took her by the elbow and ushered her into the attached room. Incongruously, it was a small library, the entrance to which was rounded and had carved into its lintel some form of text. There were four large windows on the outer facing wall, between which bookcases were built, stretching high into the ceiling and packed with books large and small. The serving girl twitched her elbow away once they were across the threshold and threw herself onto one of the low, wide settees that decorated the room.

"I thought you were a prince at first," she said. "You're not, are you?"

Rafiq was surprised into a small, coughing laugh that would have sent sparks flying in his dragon form. "I'm not a prince."

"No, you're some type of human construct." The serving girl crossed her legs, planted her elbows on her knees, and gazed at him with her chin in her palms. "Not Fae, so that's a relief. What are you?"

Rafiq stared back at her impassively, his arms folded.

She narrowed her eyes, but said: "All right, then. Something easier. What's your name?"

"Rafiq," he said.

"I'm Kako. I'm the princess' maid. Are you the prince's squire? And are you always so obedient?"

There was an expectant silence which Rafiq declined to break. It was none of this pert little serving girl's business what he was to the prince or anyone else, and his own servitude he absolutely refused to discuss.

"You don't have to answer that," said Kako, when Rafiq had made it very obvious that he wasn't going to answer. "It was a trick question anyway. I can see the link from you to him: he has you in Thrall."

Rafiq broke his silence to say: "You're a very pert maid."

"Yes," said Kako, with the air of one acknowledging a universal truth. She thought about it for a moment and added: "It's not polite to notice."

"Doesn't the princess beat you?"

"No," Kako told him. "But she's not your average sort of princess. What's your prince doing out there?"

"Thinking," said Rafiq. "He's trying to figure out all of this."

"Different from the usual type of prince, then," said Kako thoughtfully. "Does he usually oust everyone at his pleasure? No, don't strain yourself, of *course* he does."

A step at the door saved Rafiq from having to respond. Prince Akish, striding into the room, said: "Rafiq, climb out the window."

"Which window?" Rafiq asked wearily.

Kako said: "It won't do you any good."

To Rafiq's surprise, this time the prince appeared to listen to her. "Why not?"

Kako's eyes flicked toward Rafiq: he saw mischief there. "Oh well," she said: "It's easier to show you than to tell you, after all. Climb out the window, Rafiq!"

Rafiq sent her a smouldering look but since Akish didn't repeal his order, he had no other choice than to try the window. The one he chose opened easily, but upon climbing out he was somehow not at all surprised to find himself climbing back into the library via another window with no sensation of missed time. Prince Akish looked sourly crestfallen: Kako, if Rafiq read her aright, was trying not to laugh.

"You," said the prince suddenly, pointing at Kako. Her face sobered immediately: she looked distinctly cautious. "What function do you perform here?"

"Personal maid to the princess," said Kako immediately. "Your highness."

"Do you wander at will?"

"That depends, your highness. If there are no challengers in the Keep, yes. If the Circles are begun, no."

"But you know the ways through the challenges."

"Only the princess and the dragon know the way through the Circles," said Kako. "At least, they know the way through the first six Circles: no one but the Enchanted Keep itself knows the way through the Seventh Circle. I know where they are and what they look like."

"Does not the princess wander at will through the Keep?"

Kako gave that little half-shrug again. "She's under enchanted sleep most of the time, actually. When the dragon is out and about she's asleep all the time."

"To prevent her escape," nodded Prince Akish.

"How did you guess, your highness?"

"It's a clever ruse," said Akish, his chest expanding slightly. Obviously, thought Rafiq, he hadn't noticed the sarcasm in Kako's congratulatory tones. "But fairly obvious when one thinks about it."

"Oh yes," murmured Kako. "Very obvious!"

"The Keep, it's sentient?"

Kako hesitated. "No one really knows. We think it *may* be sentient, but it's only responded to three of the experiments we've performed over the years. We still don't know if it's playing with us or if the magic that made it is simply so good that it presents as sentient."

"But it's familiar with you? It recognises you?"

"As much as a building can recognise anything, your highness: yes."

The prince nodded. "Very well. We'll take you with us."

"That's very kind of you," said Kako, with a light frosting of sarcasm. And yet, Rafiq was almost certain that the prince's declaration had pleased her.

"Bivouac for the night," said Prince Akish. "We shall proceed in the morning."

Sunlight was streaming through the windows when Rafiq awoke the next morning. He rose, stretching, and prowled closer to the golden warmth of it, a purr beginning deep in his chest but unable to roll properly in his human throat. Kako was curled up on a settee in the skewed square of light from one window, a twist of pink silk against the dark green of her chosen bed. A faint marking of lines on the marble floor showed where she'd dragged the couch in order to catch the light. Rafiq frowned down at her, his thoughts troubling him. There was still something so *familiar* about her. Yet, as far as it went, there was no reason why she should be familiar. A human, a female, a Shinpoan; he had certainly never met her before. He would have remembered her, he was sure, for in the bright sunlight he could see what he hadn't seen yesterday: Kako was covered in myriad mismatching scars and scrapes. There was quite a large one along her right arm that showed soft, newly stretchy skin almost an inch wide at its widest. It made a long, tapering 'v' from her rounded shoulder to the inside of her elbow. There were a multitude of tiny cross-hatched scars across her knuckles and fingers, and the one scar that Rafiq *had* noticed yesterday was not the simple thing that it seemed. It ran across one foot, and with Kako curled as she was on the settee he could see the pad of her foot, where it made a darkened divot in the skin. Had someone tortured the girl?

Rafiq's eyes went to her face, and saw that even Kako's slightly lop-sided smile was due to a small scar that pulled at her upper lip. He thought he saw the pinkening of new scar toward the edge of Kako's neck scarf and reached out curiously to pull the scarf away.

"Marred little thing, isn't she?" said Prince Akish's voice. "Careful! Take her scarf and you'll find yourself wedded to the chit: Shinpoans are very traditional when it comes to the neck-scarf."

Rafiq's hand dropped. *"Wedded?"*

18

"Only a bridegroom can uncover his bride's neck," said the prince. "Shinpoan ladies are only permitted to cease wearing the scarf after they're married."

To Rafiq, this seemed nonsensical: he could see the girl's navel, after all! Her bodice, such as it was, covered what Illisrans would consider only to be the bare essentials, and no Illisran woman would wander her house or grounds with her midriff bare. Nor would they be seen in a pair of trousers, no matter how light and graceful they were. Dragons, now: things were much simpler with dragons. No fuss about scarves or midriffs or lengthy wedding settlements. No even lengthier schism settlements. There was a drake and his she-dragon, and they wedded for life.

Rafiq settled back onto his rug cross-legged, where he could see both the sleeping Kako and Prince Akish, who had gone into the hall to begin his morning stretches. Akish always looked distinctly peeled of a morning: stripped of his chainmail and leg armour, his bulk was considerably lessened. This morning he was stretching in preparation for his sword drill, his shadow rippling smoothly over the blood-red floor. Before long the prince would be lunging and setting, practising his strokes: a routine as familiar as it was unvarying.

Rafiq turned his attention back to the sleeping Kako. Here was an uneasiness that was tugging uncomfortably at the back of his mind– what was it about her that was so instinctively familiar? Human women were even harder to read than human men, perhaps because he saw so few of them. What was it about Kako that made her so easy to read? He was still frowningly observing Kako when her eyes opened and met his, sleepy and then sharp. She looked cautious and a little bit speculative.

Rafiq said: "You sleep very late for a serving maid."

"You're a strange little construct," she said, yawning and stretching. "It's not polite to watch people while they sleep: didn't your prince tell you that? It borders on disturbing, actually."

Rafiq was goaded into retorting: "My usual form isn't this *little.*"

"Speaking of your usual form, what is it? More importantly, why do you have fire running through the magic around you–" Kako's mouth remained open, but her words died away. She leaped from her settee and crouched in front of Rafiq, who submitted without blinking to a wide-eyed and animated scrutiny that lasted for many minutes. When at last she was done, Kako looked at him with slightly dazed eyes and said: "Rafiq, where did your dragon go?"

Rafiq crossed his arms.

"That dragon, the one who killed the Keep's dragon. Where is it?"

"It went away." It didn't sound convincing even to his own ears.

"*You're* the dragon!"

"I'm a man," said Rafiq. His voice sounded even less convincing.

Kako, her eyes shining, said: "You're the *dragon!* You're a dragon-human construct! How are you doing that?"

"He told me to be man," said Rafiq, with bitterness in his soul. "I became man."

"Yes, you're under Thrall: I understand that. But even a dragon in Thrall can't change into a man at will."

Rafiq, who knew of several ancient draconian lines whose descendants could and did change to man (or woman) at will, shrugged. When it came to consciousness, humans and dragons were not so far apart. That fact more than magical talent made the change between species possible.

Kako drew in a deep breath, questions blossoming in her eyes, but before she could speak even one of them Prince Akish strode into the room in all his sweat and said: "Up, lizard! The day has well begun. We shall seek food, and then the way forward."

"There is no food," said Kako, accepting Rafiq's offered hand to rise from the rug. "It's not part of the paradigm. Unless you'd like to eat books, of course."

Of course, thought Rafiq sourly, Prince Akish still had his rations pack: a small, half-empty skin of water and two days' worth of marching rations. Those rations, he was well aware, wouldn't be offered to him. He could go for longer than Akish without food—or water, if it came to that—but it wouldn't be pleasant.

"Water, then? How will I wash?"

"You won't. Your highness. Water isn't part of the paradigm either."

"Rafiq, seize the serving maid. Menace her with your dagger or some such thing."

Rafiq obeyed with murder in his thoughts. Kako squeaked when he folded one arm around her swiftly, pinning her arms to her sides and her back to his chest, but though she was startled she didn't seem to be frightened. She didn't even wriggle when Rafiq's dagger caught in the folds of her neck scarf.

He said, through his teeth: "I object to menacing females."

"Your objection is heard and disregarded," said Akish. "Now, maiden: inform the Keep that if it doesn't co-operate, I will slaughter you where you stand."

"You can tell it yourself, if you like," said Kako, but she nevertheless called out: "The prince says he'll kill me if you don't co-operate."

There was the kind of awkward silence that suggested everybody knew somebody had been made a fool of, but nobody quite liked to say so. Prince Akish clicked his tongue impatiently. "Ho there! Open the third Circle to us or your serving maid dies!"

Rafiq felt Kako sigh slightly. "It's not a person, your highness. It doesn't understand death. The Circles can't be cheated: threatening me will only waste time we could be using to find the way ourselves."

"Let her feel the point of the dagger," said Akish softly.

Rafiq didn't try to resist the order: his hands were less controlled when he was resisting, and he would much rather prick Kako's neck on purpose than cut her throat by accident. He heard a small, sudden intake of breath from Kako, then something liquid and hot burned his thumb and forefinger. Rafiq stiffened and looked down to find that the blade of his knife was gone. No, not gone: melted, the steel of it dripping on his fingers and burning the flesh. He took in a silent breath through his teeth and quickly wiped the burning liquid away on the shoulder of Kako's bodice, prompting the scent of scorched silk to rise faintly in the air. Her head turned as he looked down, and her eyes met his, faintly challenging.

Fortunately, Prince Akish hadn't noticed the melted blade. He was glaring around the room as if expecting attackers to leap from behind the curtains and under the books, and by the time his gaze fell on Rafiq and Kako again, Rafiq had angled the handle of the dagger so that the prince wouldn't have been able to see the blade if it *was* there.

"There's no one to save me," Kako said. Once again, her words had the ring of universally known truth. Was that, Rafiq wondered privately, because she really had no one to look after her, or because she didn't *need* anyone to look after her?

"Enough of this foolery," said Prince Akish impatiently, interrupting his thoughts. "Let the wench go, Rafiq. We've wasted enough time on this trial."

Rafiq released Kako in relief. It was bad enough that he'd killed a she-dragon. To kill a human female as well would have been a hard thing to live with, as impossible as it would have been for him to do anything about it. Kako adjusted her neck scarf with a great dignity that was only slightly ruined by the tiny, still-smoking holes Rafiq's melted blade made in the light fabric and the smell of burnt silk that still permeated the air.

"What are your instructions?" Rafiq asked the prince. In general he made it a rule not to ask for Commands: he far preferred misinterpreting those orders given him and dodging the ones that he could conveniently not hear. In this case, however, it seemed safer to direct Prince Akish's thoughts toward anything but threatening the female servants of the Keep.

"We shall search for secret passages," said Prince Akish. "A keep as big as this one must surely be bristling with hidden nooks and crannies. I'll search in the main hall: you can have the library. Don't leave any corner of the room unsearched."

As far as it went, thought Rafiq as the prince removed himself to the hall; the command was both comfortable and easy to follow. He very precisely searched the corners of the room first, while Kako watched with narrowed eyes, then investigated the corners where book-cases met walls for good measure. That did away with his Burden and left him to search in comfort and with just as much vigour as he chose to exert.

He was carelessly tipping books on their spines with the rather nebulous idea that any secret passage in the Keep would likely be activated by a bookish lever when it occurred to him to ask: "Why a library?"

"Why not?" said Kako, with her elegant half-shrug.

"I'm a dragon."

"Yes, we established that."

"Libraries don't adjoin grand halls. Or foyers."

"I see. You're saying that on your authority as a dragon." Her voice was so reasonable. Rafiq was certain she was laughing at him.

By way of explanation, he said: "If even a dragon knows it, everybody must. Why a library?"

"Well, the foyer out there isn't always *the* foyer, if you know what I mean. Sometimes the Keep likes to put another hall or foyer there instead."

"Mm," murmured Rafiq, to give himself time to think. She was only telling half of the truth. "What's written on the lintel?"

"That? It's Shinpoan. *Books are the door, but Knowledge is the key.*

It's an old saying that means a well-informed mind will learn more from a book than an ignorant one."

"Mm."

Kako's almond eyes flicked over to him and away again. "You're unusually talkative today."

Rafiq only grunted at her this time. He wasn't exactly talkative at the best of times, but he distinctly disliked being lied to, and he was certain that Kako's entire conversation with him had consisted of half-truths and misdirection. As little as Prince Akish liked being made a fool of did Rafiq like it.

Prince Akish called for a halt when the natural light faded. Neither he nor Rafiq had found a single secret passage or hidden door: just the same grand flight of stairs and the same two rooms, hall and library. Rafiq, supposedly searching the library with Kako, heard the enraged stomping of feet on the stairs as Akish's temper got the best of him and he sought determinedly to climb through as many iterations of the hall and stairs as it took for the scenery to change. It hadn't changed, of course, and the prince had eventually tired himself out enough to declare an end to the day's struggles. None of them were in a particularly good mood by then: Akish was tired and hungry, Rafiq was hungry and puzzled, and Kako's pinched face said that she was hungry too. It was rather a relief when they each turned to their own favoured sleeping spots and ignored the others in favour of sleep.

Rafiq woke in the sable dark, unsure of what it was that had roused him. He could hear the prince's heavy breathing, and to his left was the soft in and out of Kako's breath. There was nothing irregular or threatening about it. The rest of the room was silent: a heavy silence from the book-lined walls and five cold points of empty silence where the windows and connecting door made a hole in the books. Then, while Kako's breath remained soft and steady, Rafiq heard the slither as she uncurled from her settee and set her bare feet silently on the marble floor. Not asleep, then. Rafiq cracked his eyelids open just enough to see a blurred slit of the room as Kako looked, listened, and stole away softly across the swiftly cooling tiles. Where was she going? It came to his mind that she had slept late yesterday morning: had she been wandering last night as well? And if so, where? Two rooms and a staircase didn't leave a lot of leeway.

He briefly considered following her, but by the time he sat up Kako's almost indiscernible footsteps had died away altogether and Rafiq had the distinct impression that she was no longer in the two-room paradigm with himself and Akish. Besides, if he knew where she'd gone and Prince Akish asked about it later, Rafiq would have to tell him. Rafiq preferred to tell the prince as little as possible, and if he didn't know anything he couldn't tell anything.

By the time Kako returned, waking him, the pre-dawn cool was already seeping across the marble floor, causing Rafiq to burrow deeper into his rug in an attempt to escape its lingering touch. Through his eyelashes he could see that Kako was weary but well content, a glow of satisfaction about her. She fell asleep almost immediately and this time Rafiq could hear the difference in her breathing. She must have stayed awake for hours waiting for himself and Akish to fall asleep.

What exactly did she want with himself and Akish? She certainly had no need to stay with them. And when Prince Akish had declared his intention of taking her with them yesterday, Rafiq was certain that Kako had been pleased. Was she a part of the Keep's enchantments? Was she only there to obfuscate the path and hamper them in the Circles of Challenge?

IT WASN'T until quite late in the day that Prince Akish sent a bellow of triumph echoing through the two-room paradigm. Rafiq, who had been prowling the great hall—ostensibly in search of a way forward but actually in search of some form of food—betook himself to the next room slowly enough to please himself while not being slow enough to force Akish to call him in.

Kako was already there, reclining on a settee with a book and not looking very interested. Akish was standing in front of one of the emptier bookcases, his face alight with triumph, and when he drew nearer Rafiq understood why. It was curious that he and Kako hadn't seen it: those two stacks of books supporting the old shelving made a doorway.

"The writing," he said, nodding.

Prince Akish's eyes flamed. "Books are the door!"

"And knowledge is the key," agreed Kako. "It's a Shinpoan saying."

"It's a sign," Akish said impatiently. "You wouldn't understand. Those piles of books are the doorway to the next Circle."

Kako's eyes became particularly flat. "How interesting. How does that work?"

"I suppose one simply walks through it."

"I see. You don't seem to be getting very far."

Prince Akish, who had tried to walk through one rather sturdy wall, pounded his fist on the blocks that showed between book stacks. "Why isn't it working?"

"Maybe the door's shut," said Kako helpfully.

"There must be a key phrase to unlock it." Prince Akish crossed his arms tightly across his chest, scowling. *"Knowledge is the key! Books are the door!"*

"It's not working," Rafiq said, when it was obvious that it *wasn't.*

"It *must* work!" Prince Akish said furiously. "The words are a sign! My conclusions are correct!" He made a violent gesture at the wall, spewing potent magic from his fingers, and both piles of books exploded in a fluttering of leaves and covers, knocking several other books from the shelves and starting a domino effect of several massive tomes that had been leaning against the back of one of the settees. The last of these, a monstrously large and improbably thin atlas with biscuit-coloured borders that was nearly as tall as Kako, tilted ponderously and slapped against the marble floor with a soft, dusty *paf!*

All three of them stared at it speechlessly, aware of Prince Akish's magic reacting with something distinctly magical in the book before it fizzled away.

"It's certainly big enough," Kako said.

Prince Akish, recovering both his temper and his breath, ordered: "Open the book, lizard."

This time it was obvious that they'd chosen the right way. When Rafiq propped the atlas back up against a bookshelf and opened it, the internal magics lit the dusty twilight of the room. He opened it to the page that it most naturally opened at, and instead of a map they found themselves looking at a highly detailed rendering of what seemed to be another room in the Keep. It was about the size of a large ballroom, the marble tiles on the floor of myriad colours, and was rather incongruously dotted with a series of articles that looked distinctly out of place. Even to Rafiq the profusion of chairs, desks, random ottomans, and chaise lounges seemed unusual. If he wasn't mistaken, there was also the odd wardrobe or two about the room, and that was certainly a massively canopied bed over in one corner.

Prince Akish gazed at the room in mingled triumph and dissatisfaction. "Why are there articles of furniture strewn through your ballroom?"

"It's only one ballroom of many," Kako said. "I suppose it needed to keep the spare furniture *somewhere.*"

Rafiq, certain that Kako was again only telling half of the truth and rather annoyed with her in consequence, said abruptly: "Who goes first?"

"The serving girl," said Akish at once, as Rafiq had been certain he would. "I will follow her and you will immediately follow me. Do you understand?"

"I hear and obey."

"Very well. Lead the way, wench."

Kako's one-shouldered shrug as she turned away from the prince was as eloquent as an eye roll. In turning, she slipped sideways and into the room in one unconsciously familiar movement that had Rafiq wondering just how well she knew the magic of the Keep.

The prince waited only until a rather flat representation of Kako appeared on the page before he followed her through without a ripple of the sorcerous page, leaving Rafiq to bring up the rear with the rather grim question of what the third Circle would present in the way of challenge.

* * *

THE BOOK GLOWED BRIEFLY as the last of the challengers stepped through, and when the glow faded a certain swirling of unformed words remained. Slowly, slowly, word by word, two lines formed in soft sepia on the creamy page.

Herein is entry to the Perilous Room
Seek the Changeable Path or find here your Doom.

The Second Circle is ended.

4

THE THIRD CIRCLE

The first thing Rafiq heard after a fuzz of soft edges and round, fluffy noises was the sound of Prince Akish swearing. That was neither soft nor fluffy. At first Rafiq thought that the tiles beneath his feet were soft and fluffy too, but once his consciousness adjusted to the abrupt fact that he was now in the ballroom he'd seen from the book, he came to the rather unpleasant realisation that the tiles were in fact some sort of quicksand, and that he had sunk in it to his knees. Prince Akish had also sunk into the floor some way ahead of him and was making all possible speed to clamber onto a nearby table that was squat, long, and above all unsinking.

"Chair," said Kako significantly. She alone was standing on a tile that seemed to be solid, and if Rafiq read her aright, she was very much amused. Still, there *was* a chair in easy reach, and when he carefully levered himself out of the miry tiles and onto it, he found that quite a decent area around the chair seemed to be quite solid as well. It was hard to be annoyed with Kako when the floor beneath him was so blessedly normal.

Prince Akish scowled around at the ballroom. "What enchantment have we walked into?"

"I think," said Kako, with a laugh trembling in her voice; "I *think* the floor is quicksand."

"Don't be pert, girl. I could ascertain so much for myself."

"No, you don't understand," Kako said. The laugh was gone from her voice but to Rafiq's eyes she fairly irradiated laughter. "Look at all the furniture: it's just close enough to clamber on or jump to. It's a giant game of The Floor Is Quicksand. I used to play it with my brother and sisters."

Prince Akish's brows snapped together. "Is this accursed place making light of our quest?"

Rafiq cast his eyes up and began feeling carefully around the base of his chair with his feet. Once Prince Akish began to be annoyed about real or perceived slights, everything took lesser place to his ire. Still, when he finished being annoyed he was bound to tell Rafiq to find them a way forward, and since Rafiq was now hungry with the kind of dull, continuous ache that preyed upon the mind, it seemed sensible to begin finding a way through the quicksand.

"Not light, exactly," Kako said, as Rafiq's questing feet met slightly firmer tile where he was certain he had only met treacherous quicksand before. "It does seem to have a fascination with games, though."

"Rafiq–" began Prince Akish.

"Never mind Rafiq; he's stuck over there," said Kako. "I'll find a path for us."

Was he stuck, though? wondered Rafiq. The tiles that he had mired through seemed to be solidifying quite quickly.

"Stay there," Kako said warningly as Rafiq brought his feet beneath him to rise. "The quicksand is beginning to firm."

"That's a good reason to move," he said.

"Yes, if it were going to stay like that. I've got a feeling that it's only gone away to make room for something more nasty."

"What about you?"

"I think I've found a pattern," said Kako. "I'm sure I'll be fine.

Three to the left, then blue, then yellow. One step back, repeat. I tested it with the quicksand tiles before you both got here. There was a bit of a lag."

And *there*, thought Rafiq. There it was again! The strange, absolute certainty that Kako was lying to them. Still, lying or no, when she made her way across the floor toward him in an inching, crab-like manner that followed her prescription, she didn't sink so much as an inch through the tiles.

She was quite close to him when Rafiq heard the faint whirring of something magical stirring. It was deep in the floor, crawling along the underside of the tiles. Rafiq was still trying to pinpoint the source of it when Kako said a frantic: "*Aiee!*" and leapt for his lap. He caught her by reflex, wincing very slightly: for all her diminutive size, Kako was surprisingly heavy. She was also surprisingly warm for a human. Where a bare section of her back touched the inside of his arm Rafiq felt the contact like a ray of the hottest summer sun. Without meaning to, he found himself tightening his arms around Kako, delighting in the sunlight warmth of her.

She wriggled indignantly, and when Rafiq remembered himself enough to release her, she immediately curled one foot up to examine it. There was blood seeping from the underside of it. Rafiq automatically reached for the foot to inspect the damage but Kako elbowed him and hunched away, swiping the trickle of blood away on the silken fabric that clothed her other leg.

"It's fine. The wound will close by itself."

"What is it?" called the prince.

"Spikes," said Kako, observing the floor with disfavour. "Small and very sharp. Lucky I was mostly on the right path. They took me by surprise."

Surprise? wondered Rafiq. No, that was annoyance he'd seen on her face. Annoyance at herself. At her own carelessness, perhaps? And *why* could he smell burning silk once again? That was the important question, decided Rafiq. Another was the question of why Kako was so very warm? His eyes snapped to Kako's face, which was at present looking decidedly wary, a light suffusion of dark orange permeating the air around her. It was very, very faint: had been faint from the first moment he'd seen her. Those tiny, tell-tale colours in aura around her had been so close to indiscernible that Rafiq hadn't consciously seen them. He'd only reacted to them as he would have reacted to any other she-dragon.

Remembering his melted blade and the scent of burning silk then, he grimly bent to examine Kako's trouser leg in spite of her physical and verbal protests. There where her blood had smeared across the silk were burnt patches; tight, crumpled little sections that had blackened, hardened, and in some cases burnt right through.

"Happy?" said Kako when he straightened. "When I melted your stupid dagger it ruined the only set of clothes I have access to."

Rafiq looked down into those clever, wary, almond eyes and said in quiet certainty: "You have fire in your blood."

Kako startled so badly that she almost fell off his lap and into the intermittent spikes that surrounded them. She caught herself with one clutching hand at Rafiq's collar and said: "Excuse me?" Her voice was very carefully calculated between anger and annoyance, but Rafiq could see reddening in her faint aura. She was very frightened indeed. If he hadn't been sure of it before, he was now.

"Sorry," he said, and tore away the whispy loops of Kako's scarf from her neck.

She made a stifled sound, snatching the scarf back to her neck, but it was too late. Rafiq had already seen the new, pink scar that ran below her left ear and across her throat to the opposite shoulder. It was a very familiar slash: he had used the exact slice on the Dragon of the Keep.

Kako was the Dragon of the Keep.

"Don't assault the serving maid!" called the prince irritably. "I informed you of neck scarfs earlier, Rafiq. I won't be held responsible if she wants to marry you."

"We'll talk later," said Rafiq softly, as Kako rewound her scarf.

Kako, with her fingers trembling slightly, said to the prince in a careless voice: "Oh no! My mother expects me to marry much higher. At least a steward, I should think."

The prince, who didn't care about the matrimonial aspirations of a serving girl, said: "Is the path found, or must we begin again?"

"It's found," said Kako, slipping from Rafiq's lap. She favoured her left foot slightly but didn't seem to have too much trouble standing. "I just had to stop for a bit to fix my foot. Follow me, Rafiq. Three steps to the left, then blue, then yellow. One step back, repeat. Follow me exactly. And make sure your *whole* foot is inside the tile. The spikes are rather painful."

Kako and Rafiq made their way slowly across the floor, followed closely and then overtaken by the evening shadows. By and large their path bore them left, and it wasn't long before Prince Akish was cautiously able to lower himself to the floor behind them. Kako was entirely silent, and though Rafiq had found her chatter both bothersome and cheeky, he now found that he felt very badly about her muteness. It seemed, he thought uncomfortably, that he'd behaved more like Prince Akish than a dragon, and he didn't like the feeling. He didn't miss the occasional look that Kako flicked his way, her sloe eyes shuttered and watchful.

Akish, while not so self-absorbed as to be oblivious to the tension, was fortunately too busy counting tiles under his breath to notice, and it wasn't until they found themselves between a wardrobe and the grand bed they'd seen from the other Circle that he seemed to notice how little light remained of the day. He muttered something beneath his breath, producing a flare of sorcerous light, and at once the tiles beneath their feet blanched to white, all hope of identification gone.

"That's torn it," said Kako, gazing around. They were the first words she'd spoken in quite some time, and it was something of a relief to hear her voice again. Rafiq realised that he'd been waiting for her to disappear through the Door Out and leave himself and Akish to their own machinations.

Prince Akish said something rather rude and banished the light, but it was too late. In the last of the fleeting sun the tiles remained white, useless as a guide. "What happened?" he demanded.

"I think your magic reacted with the Keep's magical mechanics. It thinks you're trying to cheat with magic, so it's taken away your privileges."

The prince looked annoyed with himself. "I didn't consider the possibility. Will the patterns come back, wench?"

"I'd imagine so," Kako said. "Probably not until morning, though. We may as well stop for the night."

"What a plaguey nuisance! Very well, we'll stop for the night. Find somewhere to sleep and we'll start again in the morning."

Prince Akish of course took the bed. It was a massive, canopied thing that could have held the three of them with ease and very little embarrassment, but in spite of that Kako made herself a nest in the wardrobe with some conveniently hanging furs and Rafiq threw himself onto a nearby chaise lounge that was much less comfortable than it looked. From there he could see the diminishing flame of the sunset as it flickered and died, while listening to Kako's tiny rustles as she settled in her wardrobe and Prince Akish's various rasps, rattles and thumps as he divested himself of the more cumbersome pieces of his armour.

After the fidgets and rustles came the quiet, and it was slowly borne in on Rafiq that Kako was working small, quiet magic. He rolled over to watch her work, the soft, fiery heat of her magic

overshadowing the peaceful iridescence of lavender that fluctu-
ated in her aura. It looked as though the working was calming
her.

When Prince Akish' irregular in and out of breath had settled
down to a rhythmic snore, Kako's voice, low and muted, said:
"Are you going to tell him?"

"No," said Rafiq. "But if he asks me–"

"You'll have to tell him. All right. I can work with that."

Rafiq, struggling to find a way to put his regret into words,
rolled over onto his back once again and said to the ceiling: "I
didn't mean to tear your scarf. I'll get you a new one."

Kako's dragon aura had almost faded now, but he saw the
faint edging of forgiving gold from the depths of the wardrobe
and relaxed.

"That's all right," said Kako. "I have others. Good night, Rafiq."

Kako was gone again. Rafiq, waking late in the night to the
solitary snoring of Prince Akish, saw the empty, shadowed inside
of the wardrobe in which she'd been sleeping. He was conscious
of a feeling of relief mingled with disappointment: it was safer if
she stayed away from Akish, but he'd really thought she meant it
when she said she'd stay. He found himself regretful that he
wouldn't have the chance to ask Kako about her dragon form. He
would have liked to know more about the construct– not to
mention the small matter of why she wasn't dead. He'd never
heard of a human with fire in the blood surviving when they died
in dragon form.

Rafiq was still pondering the question when he heard slight
scuffling sounds from across the room. It was Kako; carefully
clambering across furniture piece by piece to make her way back
to the wardrobe, and she appeared to be carrying a small bundle.
It seemed good to Rafiq to close his eyes once again and feign
sleep. He was surprised to discover himself smiling.

He felt Kako hovering over him a little later. What was she
about? Then there was a slight fumbling somewhere in the

region of his right arm, and Rafiq heard the slight creak of the wardrobe as Kako climbed back in and made herself comfortable. He sat up and saw in the grey light of early morning that she had tucked a carefully folded handkerchief of food into the crook of his arm, along with a small flask of water. The food was simple fare—bread and some species of preserves that were tangy and a little bit sweet—but there was quite a lot of it. It was the sort of thing he would have expected of a hungry youth raiding the larder late at night. It was immensely satisfying; filling and delightfully piquant.

When he had finished eating Rafiq folded the handkerchief neatly, took a long, refreshing draught of water, and lay back to gaze up at the silvery ceiling with his hands laced behind his head. It was very pretty, of course, but the silver did throw some strange reflections. The blue in the floor, for example, was nothing like the blue that the silver reflected back at him. It was more of a robin's egg blue. And come to think of it, the yellow tiles reflected in the ceiling looked closer to robin's egg blue than yellow, too.

Rafiq blinked. Ah. They'd been looking for patterns in the wrong place. His eyes followed the pattern of blue across the ceiling and found that it led very precisely and easily to a window across the ballroom. Rafiq briefly considered pointing it out to Akish, but after the food and drink Kako had brought he wasn't distractingly hungry or thirsty– or particularly inclined to assist the prince, if it came to that.

Rafiq threw a look over at Kako and saw that she was watching him, her eyes glittering in the shadows. She had realised the same thing that he had; and like himself, was declining to tell the prince. Interesting. He closed his eyes and drifted back into a pleasant sleep.

THE DAY WAS one of annoyance and frustration. Prince Akish was frustrated, which meant that everyone around him was annoyed. It didn't help, thought Rafiq tiredly, that by the time Kako had led them another few feet across the tiled floor, the pattern suddenly and explicably changed. The first indication they had of any such thing was the tiles heating painfully beneath their feet. By the time they'd scrambled for somewhere safe, Prince Akish's boots were smoking gently and the soles of Kako's feet were burnt into red, angry blisters.

Kako looked more resigned than tearful, though her face had a carefully blank look that suggested she wasn't giving in to her pain. Akish, on the other hand, was loud and vituperative in his distress both of burnt shoe-leather and lost path, and spent the next few hours eating his rations in an angry sort of way before climbing over some of the closer furniture to get a better look at the room. When Rafiq asked somewhat sarcastically for Commands, Akish only said: "Be silent, lizard. I am attempting to find the pattern again."

True to his word, he *did* find the pattern again. By that time Kako had managed to heal the burns on her feet, and though the scar was still on the bottom of her foot, the rest of the skin looked smooth and new.

"How did you find it?" she asked Akish, accepting Rafiq's hand to rise from the footstool upon which she had taken refuge.

"The pattern was clear from above," said Akish grandly, and led the way.

Rafiq exchanged a look with Kako, brows raised. Akish was obviously in one of his more childish moods today. Rafiq had known him to go into terrifyingly infantile rages at the least pretext when he was in such a state, the prince's vaunted prowess and battle cunning notwithstanding. Kako looked distinctly wary and Rafiq got the impression that she was used to dealing with such anger. He wondered if her princess often went into the same kind of paroxysms.

Before long it was obvious to Rafiq that the pattern was not taking them in the direction he had discovered last night. That was unfortunate, given Akish's current mood, but he saw no reason to enlighten the prince. He was beginning to think that Kako was by no means eager for them to get through the Circles of challenge, and since it was no part of Rafiq's design to make things easy for Prince Akish, he continued to follow behind silently. The pattern ended at a small side-door at the other end of the ballroom from whence they had entered. Prince Akish, with a grunt of triumph, wrenched the door open, and an incongruous flood of late afternoon sunlight streamed into the room.

"Oh well done," said Kako. "You've found the Door Out."

Rafiq craned his neck to see around the seething Prince Akish, and found himself looking at the wide stairs and open courtyard by which he and Akish had entered the Keep.

"This," said Akish through his teeth, "Is insupportable! Wench, what is the meaning of this?"

"It's the Door Out," Kako repeated. "I told you: there's one for every Circle. We've been following the wrong pattern."

Much to Rafiq's surprise, the prince didn't immediately explode. Instead, he said: "You did inform me. This challenge is more irritating than I'd supposed. Can we go back to the entrance of this Circle?"

"We can go back to the point at which we entered, but the door is closed to us. We can only go forward or out."

"You know a great deal, wench," said Akish, closing the door again. He turned his back to it and looked very narrowly at Kako. "I'm beginning to believe I went too lightly on you in the last Circle."

"Oh, is Rafiq going to hold a knife to my throat again?"

Prince Akish put one hand around her throat almost casually. "You're remarkably forward for a maid."

"Yes," said Kako. Her voice was strained, but she was otherwise unaffected. "The princess finds it very useful."

Rafiq made a restless move, powerless by Thrall to do

anything to help; and Prince Akish, jerking Kako closer, shot him a smouldering look. "Keep back, lizard! I don't need your help. How do we proceed to the next circle, wench?"

"I'm sure we have to find the right pattern to follow," said Kako chokingly. Her face was suffused with crimson, but when Rafiq opened his mouth to tell the Prince he'd found the way himself he saw Kako's hand rise, the index finger slightly uplifted. "I don't know anything else."

"I don't believe you. You know entirely too much of this accursed place."

Kako rasped: *"Live here. Know how it thinks."*

"You'll kill her," Rafiq said shortly. Kako's finger was still raised, but she was beginning to droop. He opened his mouth to tell the prince the way out in spite of her wishes but Kako lost consciousness as he did so, dragging the prince forward with the unexpectedness of her weight. Akish gave vent to a series of unpleasant remarks regarding her parentage and said to Rafiq: "Plague take the wench, she knows nothing after all! Pick her up and carry her back with us. It's possible she may yet prove useful."

They spent the afternoon back at the bed, where Kako took far longer than she should have to regain consciousness and the prince did a piece of magic that made a fat slab of architect's paper appear, along with a winding fountain pen. It also made the colours in the floor disappear once again, which irritated the prince greatly.

Rafiq deposited Kako on the chaise-lounge and removed himself to a nearby chair, worried by the amount of time that she spent unconscious until he saw her eyes open a slit to watch Prince Akish's busily moving pen as it scrawled characters and numbers on the paper slab.

He found himself grinning. How much of her faint had been real? None of it, he was inclined to think. He was also inclined to think that she'd deliberately needled the prince. There was no excuse for the prince's behaviour, of course, but Kako had seen his mood and deliberately provoked him, Rafiq was certain. What did she have to gain from being physically attacked?

When Kako finally deigned to wake from her self-imposed 'faint', the prince was still at his scribblings and Rafiq was amusedly watching her. She caught his eye and winked, then produced an entirely convincing, throbbing cough.

"Not dead, then, I see," said the prince, without looking up. "If I were you, I would begin to think of ways in which to be very useful. Your unhelpfulness is starting to pall."

"Oh," said Kako, her voice slightly raspy. "How awful. Did you know that the colours in the floor have disappeared again?"

"Yes," the prince said sourly. "I worked some magic again and the Keep took exception to it."

"I see. Just trying to be helpful."

Akish violently scribbled out a section of his figures and barked at Rafiq: "Instead of smirking, lizard, why don't you clamber over the furniture to see how far you can get?"

"Of course," said Rafiq, his grin just a little wider.

"The Floor Is Quicksand!" sang Kako at him, and leapt from the chaise lounge to a nearby desk with surprising lightness of foot. Rafiq followed her, enjoying the feel of his muscles coiling and uncoiling. There was less exercise to be had as a human, and the fact that his arms were more useable as a human never quite made up for the fact that he was always flexing his shoulders in expectation of being able to use his wings.

They enjoyed an afternoon of childish fun while the prince worked at his figures. Rafiq, chasing Kako over couch-back and under chandelier, saw Akish frequently flopping on his back on the bed and wondered that the prince didn't see the same patterns on the ceiling that he had seen.

Kako, noticing the direction of his gaze, stopped for a brief moment atop a dressing table and said: "It's the canopy. It's not just a curtained bed, it's a fully canopied one. All he can see is drapes."

Rafiq gave a hiss of laughter. "Akish was never one for sleeping with his troops."

"Exactly," said Kako. "Serves him right for taking the most comfortable bed."

"So you *do* know the way through this Circle!"

"Oh yes," Kako said, dropping lightly to the next piece of furniture by way of the chandelier. "I told you: I know the way this place thinks. I didn't think you'd figure it out, actually."

"He will, too," Rafiq warned her. "Eventually."

"Yes, but will he do it before he runs out of food?"

It was a good question, Rafiq thought. The prince was clever, but he was used to commanding battles and planning raids, not solving puzzles that seemed ridiculously complicated while being actually quite simple. The Keep's puzzles so far had been children's games– right down to the dragon that guarded it; a child's story if ever there was one. What chiefly interested him now, though, was whether Kako was a part of the Keep's magic, or whether she was an actual person.

That night when Kako carefully sneaked away, Rafiq was awake to follow her. She took a perilous route across a spaced-out series of armchairs that made a wandering line around furniture and finally came to a halt beside a knight that was guarding a shallow, curtained alcove. Rafiq, following her, discovered that the alcove became somewhat less shallow the closer one grew. By the time he was leaping from the second-last armchair to the last he could see down the alcove's gloomy length as if it was a hall. A flutter of pink silk was just disappearing around a corner at the end of it. Rafiq made short work of the last armchair, springing lightly and silently into the alcove, and hurried after Kako. Now that he had been human for a few days his native lightness of foot was growing, just as Kako's she-dragon aura faded further with each day that she didn't turn dragon.

The hall made an abrupt end in heavy curtains that were just barely parted. Rafiq had already felt the fiery magic that formed it, and if he had a guess, he would have said that Kako had joined the Keep to a room quite far away from it by the simple expedient of matching drapes.

Carefully twitching the curtains back a little more, he took a cautious look around the room. It wasn't a small one, but it looked distinctly crowded. Part of that impression was created by the sheer amount of books that had been crammed into the bookcases, corners, spare chairs and tables; but the fact that every chair not occupied by piles of books was occupied by a human of varying size, age, and sex didn't help the room to look any less crowded. There was a boy sitting solemnly on a footstool with a book that was bigger than he was lying open on his crossed legs. On the top shelf of one of the bookcases was a very tiny girl alternately turning pages and tucking strands of hair behind her ear, from whence they immediately escaped again; and the fattest two-seater couch that Rafiq had ever seen was occupied by an older girl who evidently had no idea of the way that couches worked. She was sprawled on the seat with a book resting on her stomach, her hair hanging over the side and her legs resting comfortably against the back of it, crossed at the ankles. She was showing off a good deal more light brown skin than even Shinpoans would consider to be suitable.

Across from her, as if in direct reproof, sat an elegant young woman with a gracefully straight back and correctly covered legs, reading something decorative and most likely poetical.

When Kako walked into the room, each one of them looked up, smiles—and in the case of the tiny girl in the bookcase, squealing excitement—immediately in evidence. Even the girl sitting upside down on the couch, with her clever, sarcastic face, grinned briefly.

"I see you've all sneaked out of bed again," said Kako, in a congratulatory kind of way.

"Did you make it to the third Circle?" asked the boy, his eyes bright and interested. "We've been tracking your progress on the map Dai's drawing."

"We did," Kako said. "Where's mum?"

"Probably restocking the pantry after you raided it last night," said the boy. He looked vaguely reproachful. "Why didn't you wake us?"

"I wanted to speak to mum," said Kako. "Besides, I saw you all two nights ago. And mum was the one who gave me the sandwiches, so there."

"You've tracked something nasty in," suddenly said the girl with her legs propped against the back of the couch. She nodded toward Rafiq, who *had* thought that he was sufficiently well hidden, and he found himself under the gaze of five pairs of eyes. "How unfortunate. It'll probably get stuck in the carpet, too."

Kako said: "Bother! What are *you* doing here?"

"I followed you."

"Well, yes; that's pretty obvious. I suppose you'd better come in. It's not a good idea to spend too much time in the corridor: it doesn't really exist."

"Dai!" hissed the older, elegant girl. "Cover your legs!"

The girl called Dai looked Rafiq over once boredly and said: "It doesn't matter. He's only a human-form thing. What does he care about legs?"

"Legs are full of flavour and wonderfully chewy," said Rafiq. "Also humans can't run away if you bite them off."

There was a soft *plop* as Dai's legs hit the couch and a slight scuffle as they folded beneath her. Rafiq took a certain amount of satisfaction in the fact that her eyes were now very wide and suddenly no longer bored.

"This is Rafiq," Kako said, her eyes dancing. "He's the Contender's um...servant. He's a dragon-human construct."

"Sort of the opposite of you," said the boy. His eyes weren't quite as obviously Shinpoan as the others': not only were they

43

bright blue, there was only a slight suggestion of slanting to them. "Do you eat, construct?"

Rafiq's eyes met Kako's briefly. He said: "Yes. Not as much as a human-born, but I do require some sustenance."

"Now that's interesting!" the boy said excitedly. "Kako doesn't, you see. Where do you keep your dragon form?"

"Keep it?"

He nodded expectantly. "Yes, while you're in a Constructed human body. Kako hides in wardrobes and under beds."

Rafiq looked from one to the other, frowning. "I don't...I *change*. There's no other body. First I'm dragon, then I'm man."

There was an immediate explosion of excited interest all over the room.

"But *Kako* says–"

"Kako has–"

"How do you–"

Kako, above the general hubbub, said sharply: "Enough! Rafiq isn't interested in how I change from human to dragon–"

"I am," objected Rafiq, but she ignored him.

"–he's interested in eating. Zen, why don't you get him something to eat?"

"All right, but Akira's used all of the preserves for that–"

"–for our cousin?" said Kako swiftly.

There was a brief pause while Zen pushed up his glasses and Dai chuckled.

"Yes. Our cousin ate all the preserves. I hope they give him stomach cramps. But there's a nice pie in the cooler if Rafiq would like that."

"Pie!" said a small voice immediately. Rafiq looked up and found that the diminutive girl in the bookcase was watching him intently. She'd gone back to her book when the conversation had turned to Rafiq, but the mention of pie had once more awoken her interest in the conversation. "Pie for me!" she crowed.

"Pie for Rafiq," corrected Zen, obediently closing his book and leaving the room.

"Pie for *me!*" insisted the child irritably. She abandoned her book to climb out of the bookcase backwards, and Rafiq, who instinctively moved closer when her tiny legs flailed for the next shelf, was just in time to catch her before she fell.

"It's all right, she bounces," said Dai languidly.

"Dragon!" said the child happily, wrapping her arms around Rafiq's neck. "Dragon for me!"

Kako grinned. "I thought you wanted pie?"

"Pie for me, too!"

"This is Miyoko," Kako said, by way of introduction. "Oh, and that's Suki. Akira isn't here at the moment. Zen is the one fetching the pie, and Dai is the one on the couch."

A pair of big brown eyes lit with excitement. "Fire!"

"No fire!" said Kako immediately. "Dai, did you give Mee matches again?"

"Suki took them off her days ago and I've been locking the door to my workroom."

"Don't need matches," Miyoko explained. "Dragons go *whoof!*" She puffed her cheeks out and huffed a short, slightly damp breath into Rafiq's face, by which he understood that she wished him to breathe fire. An interesting idea—could he transform enough to be able to breathe fire without needing to change all the way?—but since Zen was just staggering into the room with a tray piled high with food while Kako peeled Miyoko's arms from his neck, he didn't attempt it.

"Help yourself," Kako told him, nodding at the tray. "And quickly, too, or there'll be none left for you."

Rafiq did so hungrily; but he wasn't so eager for food that he didn't notice her pulling Dai aside to murmur in her ear. He accepted the pie Zen offered him before Miyoko could snatch it away with her tiny, grubby fingers, and watched them both out of the corner of his eye. Did something change hands? He thought so. So Kako wasn't here merely to see her family: she'd come with a purpose. Was that purpose behind why she still wandered the Enchanted Keep with himself and the prince? It was useless to attempt to hear what Kako and Dai were saying: Zen was determined to know about Rafiq's dragon form and how he changed, and Miyoko was just as determined to have Rafiq's attention all to herself. Suki tried to keep them both in some semblance of politeness, and in so doing added another layer of noise to the babble. By the time both children had been more or less quieted by their elder sister, Kako and Dai were descending upon the supper tray to snatch up the remaining crumbs that hadn't already been consumed with great dispatch by the younger two and even the lady-like Suki.

Rafiq continued to watch them thoughtfully as he ate, prompting Dai to wink at him salaciously.

Kako didn't react to his steady regard, but when he'd finished eating she said: "We'd best be going back now, Rafiq."

There was a general chorus of protest.

"But you just *got* here!"

"Pies and fruit nectar, that's all we are to you!"

"Kakooooo!"

"But Akira will be here soon, Kako!"

"I know," said Kako, answering the most comprehensible of the wails. "But I got to see Akira last night. And why else would I come to see you all but for the food and drink?"

To Rafiq's surprise, her siblings seemed to take this in good part. Zen and Miyoko crowded close to hug her around the waist and the leg respectively, and Suki sighingly kissed her cheek.

Dai gave her a sideways smile and threw herself onto a couch, blowing Kako a kiss. "Will you be back tomorrow?"

"I think so," said Kako. She and Dai exchanged a glance, and she added: "I'll want to see how you and Zen are going with that project."

Zen looked startled. "We've got a project?"

Dai roused herself enough to clip his ear with one hand. "Of course we do, you stupid squib!"

"Oh, *that* project," Zen said, his eyes sliding away from Rafiq. "All right: 'night Kako."

Kako ushered Rafiq on ahead of her, stopping only to detach Miyoko from her leg, and they walked the passage that wasn't really there in silence, all the way back to the Enchanted Keep.

THE NEXT MORNING the colour was still gone from the tiles. Rafiq, who woke with a smile on his lips and many questions bubbling in his mind, cast his eye over the tiles and snuffed a small laugh.

"Oh, are the tiles still white?" said Kako sympathetically, from her wardrobe.

"Plague take it!" Akish said angrily. "Why aren't the colours back?"

"I expect the Keep is trying a bit of negative reinforcement," Kako said, her eyes bright. She uncurled from the wardrobe with the unconscious grace of a she-dragon and stretched on the tips of her toes. "It really doesn't like having to repeat itself. I wouldn't use any more magic while you're here, if I were you."

That was moderately interesting, thought Rafiq, edging slightly sideways to make room for Kako to sit down beside him. He could have sat up, but it looked like Akish was settling to have a temper tantrum, and Rafiq didn't feel that a tantrum merited his full attention when he could recline comfortably for the duration.

"There's always the Door Out," said Kako, with the sighing weariness of one who knows she will not be attended to. Rafiq smiled up at the ceiling.

"We will not abandon the quest!" Prince Akish said immediately. "Rafiq, what do you see?"

The Burden of his Thrall fell immediately, suffocatingly vice-like. Rafiq said, as casually as he could manage: "I see the silver ceiling and the reflected patterns from the floor."

"The *patterns?*" Prince Akish stared at him, then up at the ceiling with fierce exultation. "Rafiq, find me a mirror!"

Rafiq rolled languidly to his feet, conscious of a galling annoyance at himself. He had hoped to be able to keep his own counsel better. He brought back one of the side mirrors from the dressing-table a few tiles away and passed it to Akish, meeting Kako's eyes as he did so. She did her one-shouldered shrug and smiled slightly, which made him feel better.

"*Now* we progress!" said Prince Akish exultantly, and led the way across the tiles. It was astonishingly quick once they knew the way: a bare twenty yards, and straight as an arrow to that one window. The prince hauled at the window himself, for once too eager to order Rafiq to do it, and leaned out into the open air to scout out the next Circle.

"It's a garden," he said. "Not much to be seen from here, I'm afraid. Proceed, lizard."

* * *

SOMEWHERE FAR AWAY FROM the Enchanted Keep, Dai, sister of Kako, turned a shard of sword between her fingers.

"What is it?" asked Zen. He was gazing at it with intense attention, as if he could force it to give up its secrets by the force of his will alone.

"It's part of a sword."

"I know *that*. I meant, what's it *for?*"

"Then you should have asked that," said Dai. "I don't know what it's for. Neither does Kako, but she must be trying to find out, because she wants a passable copy to replace the original. Can you do it?"

"Probably," said Zen. "Think it belongs to the prince, or Rafiq?"

"Weeeeeeell–"

"What, Kako didn't tell you?"

"Oh, she told me. Says she picked the prince's pocket. But this magic– it's *good* magic. I mean, *really* good: lovely, benevolent stuff, and is it ever *strong*! What's Akish of Illisr doing with something this nice?"

"Something nasty, belike," said Zen. "Oh! Dai! Why's your necklace doing that?"

"What? Oh!"

"That's your fae necklace, isn't it? What's it doing, trying to get away from the shard?"

"I think so," said Dai, feeling for the pendant doubtfully. It had pulled itself as far away from the shard as it could get, and now it tugged at the chain around her neck from somewhere over her shoulder. "Do you know, I'm almost certain we have a book about this. Wait here. *Don't* touch it."

Zen waited after she left the room, his hands shoved into his pockets and jiggling on his feet. It looked as though he was physically restraining himself from touching the shard. Dai returned moments later and shot him a suspicious look, but his impatience convincing her that he'd done as he was told, she wiggled the book at him.

"I was right. We *do* have a book about it. Here, hold the shard."

"All right!" He held it while Dai grew a spiky, tight-knit spell in the palm of one hand, and stood without flinching as she hurled it at the shard between his fingers. Magic hit shard, and the room lit with a flash of searing white light as the spell exploded into extinction.

"Oooooh," said Zen, his eyes bright and dazzled.

Dai grinned: a brilliant, triumphant grin. "Ah," she said. "So *that's* what it does! I think Kako is going to like this."

The Third Circle is ended.

5

THE FOURTH CIRCLE

*R*afiq dropped into the courtyard below. There were flagstones beneath his feet, cracked and ancient with weeds, and the garden in the centre of the courtyard was encroaching upon the stone border. Where once there must have been a full three yards between garden and courtyard wall, the trees now brushed against the wall. Rafiq turned to help Kako through the window and set her down gently on the flagstones, considerably puzzled. The view from the other windows had shown them to be several stories high in the Keep, and there had certainly been no sign of a courtyard garden from any of them.

Prince Akish dropped from the window behind them and looked around critically. "At least we can see the sky again! I began to fear we'd never get out of that accursed place."

Kako, looking very wary, lightly touched the courtyard wall. "I wouldn't relax just yet, your highness. This feels more perilous than the proper inside of the Keep."

"That's because it's Faery," said Prince Akish dismissively.

Kako's eyebrows twitched together. "You've been in Faery before?"

"Of course. We're allied with Faery."

"You *allied* with them? Why would you ally yourself with them?"

"Watch your impertinent mouth, wench," said Prince Akish. "The Fae are providing us with arms and spells in return for temporary land grants and safe passage for their exiles through our lands."

Kako muttered something that sounded like "*Exiles!*" with a bitter kind of mockery. "Yes, the Fae approached Shinpo about accepting some of their exiles as well. We began to allow a few through a tear between here and there because it seemed they were under attack by another group of Fae known as the Guardians. Unfortunately, those *exiles* turned out to be High Fae who took control of the towns in which they were settled and subjugated the local population into slaves. We still haven't managed to rescue all of our people, and I hear that Llassar is almost entirely over-run with Fae. A human there is no more than a dog."

"Shinpo, like Llassar, is weakly and prone to invasion," said the prince. "Illisr has not agreed to house exiles out of the goodness of its heart, it has accepted exchange for exchange. We've not weakened ourselves, we've taken advantage of the situation. Faery is indebted to us."

Rafiq, who knew something of how Faery paid its debts, exchanged a look with Kako. She was breathing fast and short, her eyes dark, and it occurred to him that this was the most openly genuine feeling he'd ever seen from her except when in the presence of her family. Almost every other word, smile or response had been carefully calculated to draw the desired reaction from Prince Akish or Rafiq himself. To what end, Rafiq still hadn't determined.

"Take to the air, Rafiq," said Prince Akish. "I'd like to know what we're working with."

"Coming?" Rafiq asked Kako. He had the distinct pleasure of seeing her completely taken aback, her eyes fearful of what he was about to say, before he added: "I can take passengers if you're not afraid to fall off."

Kako gave a tiny choke of laughter and said: "All right, then."

"You'd better get on my back now," said Rafiq. "It's going to get a bit crowded when my wings come out."

From the air the walled garden below looked distinctly small. Rafiq, circling lazily in the bright summer sun with the tiny weight that was Kako on his back, felt chilled despite the sun. There was no sign of the Enchanted Keep at all: the garden made its own solitary square against an unending plain of rolling green. The sky itself felt alien, the breeze shifting in an infinitesimally different manner than Rafiq was used to.

"It *is* Faery," said Kako in his ear, her voice stifled with unease. It was unusually easy to hear her: the rush of wind that should have been sweeping past Rafiq's ears at the speed of his flight didn't make a sound here. The unnerving silence made his scales ache in unease. To take his mind off his disquiet, he said: *-You're familiar with Faery?-*

"Not exactly," said Kako. "But the princess likes me to stay current with my studies in magic, and a knowledge of fae magic and Faery is useful."

-Do your brother and sisters practise?-

"You've been with Prince Akish a long time, haven't you?" asked Kako, after a small pause. That was interesting. She was willing to put her own secrets in his keeping, but not those of her family. Rafiq was inclined to think that her reticence meant at least one of her siblings practised magic.

-Almost as long as I remember- he said, willing to humour her. After all, it was due to him that they were now in the Fourth Circle. *-Why?-*

"Well, you're inured, aren't you? You've given up."

Rafiq was conscious of an unpleasant twisting in his stomach. *-I haven't given up!-*

"Of course you have," said Kako. "You wriggle around things and make as much of a nuisance of yourself as possible because you know you'll never escape. It's the only way you have of fighting back."

It wasn't true, thought Rafiq, dipping into the wind. It *wasn't* true. He still thought of escape and freedom sometimes. But when the old king had handed him over to Akish, the very first set of Commands the young prince gave Rafiq were ones that his father the king had passed on to him. Rafiq wasn't to injure or bring about the injury of Prince Akish. He was never to murder, or bring about the murder of Prince Akish. He was never to collude with those conspiring to bring about the murder or injury of Prince Akish.

The list of Commands was both extensive and comprehensive, and Rafiq had never found a loophole in them.

He said: *-I haven't given up-* again, and circled lower for landing.

"Well?" demanded Prince Akish when they landed and Rafiq was once again human.

"We're stranded," said Rafiq shortly. "Nothing around us but walls and grass."

"It's definitely Faery," Kako said. "Not this bit we're in, but out there. It's like a little mushroom of the human world has sprouted up in Faery."

"What happened to the Keep?"

"I think we're still technically *in* it," said Kako. "This room is just a bit leafier than a regular one."

Prince Akish said: "I found a door in the wall further on, but it's the Door Out. The rest is merely garden– and not so much of it, either. It's barely fifty yards across."

"Anything edible?" asked Kako casually.

Rafiq found it hard not to grin. Was she trying to get Akish to eat potentially dangerous Faery food?

"Some fruit: a few nuts. Nothing that doesn't look human. Better yet, there's a spring in the centre of the garden: we won't lack for food or drink while we're here."

"That's all right," said Kako; "But if there's only one door, how do we get on?"

"Over the wall, I suspect," said Prince Akish.

"The *wall*?" Rafiq repeated, startled. "You're going to go into Faery?"

"*We're* going to go into Faery," corrected Akish. "You don't think I'm going to leave you safe and warm here in the garden while I wander Faery alone, do you?"

Kako sighed. This made the prince look sharply at her.

"What is it, wench?"

"Oh, nothing. Nothing at all."

"Speak!"

"Oh well, if you want to get stuck in Faery, that's your business," said Kako. "But if you're going over the wall, I'm staying here, thank you very much."

"Come now, it's not *so* perilous!" protested the prince.

"Well, it depends who you are," Kako said. "But what it all really comes down to is that over the wall is the same thing as a Door Out, except you'll be out in Faery instead of out in the human world."

Rafiq gazed at her long and hard. Kako wanted them out of the Keep, he was certain. That being the case, why was she trying so hard to stop the Prince from climbing over the wall and into Faery? If what she said was true, once Prince Akish and Rafiq were lost in Faery, they wouldn't be able to come back.

Kako's eyes flicked up to meet his and slid away again. "In any case, you wouldn't be able to get back to the human world. Your highness. But then, you seem to be quite comfortable with the fae, so it's entirely up to you."

Prince Akish scowled down at her. "Very well: we'll separate and explore the garden. Reconvene at the spring in the centre in half an hour."

Kako immediately vanished into the shrubbery, which made Rafiq wonder more than ever what she was up to. The prince was making a direct line for the footpath that ran around the outside of the garden, so Rafiq followed Kako into the foliage, where he soon lost her among the leaves with such a thoroughness that he suspected she was using magic to avoid him. Since he didn't choose to lose her, he spent some time trying to seek out and follow her magic. This was less successful than he'd hoped: Kako seemed to have a considerable enough talent at magic to be able to hide the fact that it was considerable, and Rafiq couldn't even catch a trace of it. He spent a little time making a grid of the small garden, but when even that didn't turn up more than a brief flicker of pink scarf he took a slightly circuitous route to the spring at the centre of the garden. He'd seen it from the air earlier, and the gentle trickling sound it made meant it was easy to find through the foliage. The sound of running water also made him realise how thirsty he'd become after his short burst of dragon-ness, and by the time he did find the spring, Rafiq was parched enough to kneel by the water and scoop up frustratingly small sips of water in his cupped palm.

When his thirst was sated there was still no sign of Akish or Kako, and Rafiq felt it good to prowl closer to the garden walls. He could smell a fresh breeze sweeping over the wall, pleasantly tinged with half-familiar scents: it seemed to promise freedom. He was right at the wall before he knew it, his palms pressed against the brickwork as if he could force his way through to Faery, and a wild frustration taking hold of his soul.

Why was he always to be caged? Why could he never be free?

The spring water bubbled in his stomach, frothy and light, and the idea grew in him that he *could* be free: *would* be free. All he needed to do was climb over this wall– this cumbersome, confining wall.

Rafiq threw himself at the brickwork, silent and savage, and climbed. He heard a babble of noise that meant nothing, a mere birdcall of nonsense that tried to pluck at his reason and return it to him. Pink fluttered in his peripheral and made dashes at him, then hit him solidly, knocking him from his hold. Fire and rose dashed into the dirt together. He groaned and tried to draw breath, but the someone who had knocked the breath from his lungs was now sitting on his chest and unceremoniously shoving her fingers down his throat. Rafiq choked; retched. Pink silk tumbled off his chest as he spasmed and jerked sideways to empty the contents of his stomach in the dirt.

"That's better," said the pink silk encouragingly, when the worst of it was over.

"No," said Rafiq in a thick voice, lurching to his feet again with a dog-like determination. The pink silk seemed to tangle his legs and shove at his shoulders, and he found himself tumbling into the dirt again. He scrabbled to right himself, shaking his head to clear away the strange fog that clouded it, and heard a voice that made him struggle the more determinedly for the wall.

"What ails him? Down, you son of a lizard!"

"Oh, be *quiet!*" said the pink silk despairingly. "Can't you see you're making him worse? Look, help me tie him to the tree."

There was a frosty kind of silence while Rafiq attempted a fumbling ascent of the wall and was once more dragged back. Then the hated voice said: "I've Commanded him to lie down. Why isn't he obeying?"

"He drank water from Faery," said the pink silk. "I don't know how they got it in here, but it's Faery all right; and it's at least strong enough to give a Thrall spell fair fight if the Thrall Commands are opposed to the desire to climb over the wall."

"Why hasn't he changed back to his dragon form?"

"I'm not sure he's thinking clearly enough for that," the pink silk said seriously. Somehow or other she was twined around his wrists just as she'd twined around his ankles earlier, and that coupled with the stronger, metallic presence that hove him sideways, compelled Rafiq back into the garden against his will. He felt the wall receding from him and fought doggedly to get back, but there was no resisting the twin power of metal and silk, and before long Rafiq began to feel the tug of another wall.

"Careful, or you'll have him going for one of the other walls," said one of the voices. And then, as Rafiq felt himself spiralling down into heavy darkness, he was shoved against something hard and rough, his legs collapsing under him.

The first thing that Rafiq became aware of was the sad, aching desire to be gone from this prison and over the wall into Faery. That was a very odd thought for him to have, so he considered it carefully with his eyes closed. While he was considering it he became aware of a second sensation: that of a light breeze playing across his bare toes. Why were his toes bare?

That particular question led on to the certainty that it wasn't a breeze playing across his toes. No, somebody was *tickling* him. Something light and quick stroked across the pad of his foot, causing his toes to curl instinctively. Rafiq's eyes snapped open.

"Oh, you're awake," said Kako.

"Why are my boots gone?"

"I actually thought you'd ask why you're tied up, first," she said.

"I suppose I tried to go over the wall," Rafiq said impatiently. "Why are my boots gone?"

"I took them off," Kako said. "I wanted to see if you're ticklish."

"You wanted to see if I'm *ticklish*?"

"Yes," she said. "You are, by the way."

"It was the water, was it?"

Kako nodded. "I checked it quickly while you were uncon-scious. Faery water is being pumped into the garden through the spring."

Rafiq grimaced slightly. He couldn't help feeling that it was thoughtless of him to have taken water from inside the Enchanted Keep without even testing for residual magic first. How long had he been unconscious? It was now night, but the moon shone so brightly that it was hard to tell the time.

"Don't feel too badly about it," said Kako, as if reading his mind. "There's also a glamour on it. It's supposed to draw you in."

"Did you know?"

"What? No, of course not!"

"Do you know the way out?"

"You're very curious tonight," Kako said, looking at him through her eyelashes.

"Why didn't you want Akish and me to go over the wall?"

"As it happens, I *do* know the way out," she said. "Well, to a certain extent. I know what's required to get us through the Circle. These last four circles are the hardest: they're not so much about solving puzzles as they are about testing character."

Rafiq's chest expanded against his bonds in a huff of a laugh. If the last four circles were tests of character, Akish had no chance at all of making it through them.

"Exactly," said Kako. "These few circles should be interesting."

Interesting was one way to put it, thought Rafiq; but there was still a curl of amusement to the corner of his mouth. He flexed uncomfortably against his bonds, and said: "When are you going to untie me?"

"Not for quite a while yet," said Kako. She sounded slightly apologetic. "You've moved toward the west wall more than two inches since we've been talking."

Rafiq stared at her, then down at the dirt around the tree he was tied to. There was a distinct pattern of shuffled dirt from where he had been to where he now sat. "How long will the effects last?"

"Possibly until morning," she said. "You threw up most of it, but some of it was already in your system. When Dai ate a Faery plum it took a week to purge it– though she ate the whole thing, of course."

"Of course she did," said Rafiq, with gloomy understanding. It was obviously going to be a long night. "You might as well get some sleep."

"I'm not going to sleep," Kako said, surprised. "You'd be over the wall and away before we could get up tomorrow. I've already had to re-tie your hands three times while you were unconscious."

There didn't seem to be much to say to that, especially since the information made Rafiq realise that the muscles in his shoulders were tight, his wrists straining against whatever it was Kako had tied them with. "What did you tie me with?"

"There wasn't much to work with," said Kako, with her one-shouldered shrug. "You have two of my handkerchiefs around your wrists, and the prince used a few of his sashes around your waist and shoulders."

Rafiq found himself grinning. "Resourceful of you."

"He's not very happy about it, by the way. Apparently all his sashes have a meaning and none of them are to be used lightly. He explained them all to me but I got bored and stopped listening."

"When do you get bored and stop listening to me?" asked Rafiq curiously.

"You don't say enough to get boring," Kako said. "And quite honestly, you're more inclined to be horribly startling than boring."

Rafiq tried not to look as pleased as that made him feel. He said: "You're more inclined to lie to me than you are to tell the truth, so I suppose we're even."

"Oh!" said Kako, looking hurt. Her dragon aura had vanished completely and it was hard to tell if she was really hurt or not. Rafiq had just come to the conclusion that she really *was*, and that he ought to apologise, when she began to laugh. "Your straight face is wonderful!" she said. "All right, let's play a game. I'll answer a question truthfully for every question that you answer truthfully. Neither of us will get any sleep tonight, after all: we may as well entertain ourselves."

"How will I be able to tell if you're lying?" said Rafiq cautiously.

Kako shrugged. "You don't seem to have much trouble reading me," she said. "Guess!"

"All right," Rafiq said. "But I get to ask the first question."

"Fine," Kako said. "But if I find you too close of a questioner, I'll dissolve into tears. Just a friendly warning."

Rafiq, distracted by the thought that he hadn't yet seen Kako cry despite the roughness with which Prince Akish had attacked her, and Rafiq's own violence toward her, said: "Did you cry when you got those scars?"

"I cried for one of them," said Kako. "My turn."

"No!" said Rafiq, startled. "That wasn't my question!"

"Too late now," Kako said. "You asked, I answered. My turn!"

Rafiq eyed her broodingly. "You tricked me. You distracted me just as I was about to ask my question."

"How did you become chattel of Prince Akish?" she asked, acknowledging his accusation with a narrowing of her eyes in amusement. "I mean, Illisr is magically inclined and always up to date with the latest spells, but your Binding is something else entirely. I've never seen anything half so strong."

Rafiq's head jerked up. "What do you mean, *see*?"

"This is *my* question," Kako objected. "I answered yours. Where did he get such a spell?"

"That's two questions," said Rafiq. "You'll have to answer two questions if I answer them both."

Kako's brown eyes widened. "Finagler! All right then, I will: but you first."

"Akish had the spell from his father: I was given to him for his sixteenth birthday. His father captured me when I was a young drake, with a spell so sharp and strong I couldn't fight it. Of the spell itself I know little: the prince always said it was fae magic, but it doesn't feel like it. Strong and foreign, yes: fae, no."

"*Very* strong," said Kako absently. She was teasing one of the tattered ends of her neck-scarf between her fingers, making a longer tail-end of frayed silk.

Rafiq was hit with a sense of alienness and familiarity all at once. Kako's dragon form had the same slit eyes that looked quietly and a little slyly on the world, giving away very little; but her human form in all its strangely pleasant alienness still made the hairs rise at the nape of his neck.

"I only once heard the king speak of the spell directly," he said, hunching his shoulders slightly to curb the feeling. "It was when he gave me to Akish. He said the spell was a burden not to be taken lightly, and that many protections were bound up in it."

Kako's eyelashes dropped over her eyes as she looked down at the scarf she was playing with. Rafiq was certain he hadn't imagined the sudden glow to them, but when she looked up again her face was bland.

"Did the king mention where *he* got it?"

"That's another question," said Rafiq, with the suspicion of fire and smoke in his voice.

"So it is," said Kako. She sounded surprised. "How badly behaved of me! What would you like to ask me?"

"I have two questions," he said, unwilling to allow her to slither out of her obligations.

Kako said: "Pushy!" but she didn't seem to be offended. "Go on, then."

"How did you stay alive when I killed you?"

"Hm. I was actually hoping you wouldn't ask that."

"Why?" asked Rafiq; and then, realising his mistake: "No, that's not my question!"

"You have a lot to learn about this game," said Kako happily. "I stayed alive when you killed me because I haven't got the kind of fire in my blood that you're used to. When I change to dragon I keep my human form as well: my human body falls into a deep sleep while my consciousness goes into my Constructed dragon form. And I was hoping you wouldn't ask because I was afraid the answer would inadvertently give away something else I don't particularly want you to know."

"What–"

"And before you ask, you've used up both your questions, and I won't answer any questions asking exactly *what* I don't want you to know."

Rafiq glared at her. "Why not?"

"Because there are some things I don't want you to know," said Kako, perfectly logically. "Also, I make the rules for this game, so I'm allowed to change them when I want to."

"Does that mean I can refuse to answer questions too?"

"Of course," she said. "When we've both refused to answer three questions each, the game is over. *My* turn, I think!"

The game was a pleasant way to spend the night. Rafiq was so caught up in trying to ask the right questions and in studying Kako to guess if she was lying to him, that he didn't notice the sun was coming up until Prince Akish appeared, pulling uncomfortably at his chainmail.

"Is the lizard well again?" he said briefly.

"I think so," Kako said. "He stopped fidgeting with the handkerchiefs an hour or so ago, and he's been leaning back against the tree for the better part of half an hour. It should be safe to untie him now."

"Good," said Akish. "I've solved this Circle while you were twittering away together. Untie him."

Kako said agreeably: "How nice!" and untied Rafiq, who

hadn't realised that she'd been watching him– or that he hadn't had the desire to climb over the wall in quite some time now.

"What's the solution?" he asked Akish, while Kako's fingers tickled around his wrists.

"The water is fae water," said Akish, his eyes gleaming. "And when I went around the garden this morning I noticed that there were some fae plants here as well. In fact, they're *all* fae plants: every morsel of food or sustenance to be had in this accursed place is fae and inedible to us."

"I'm sure they are if you say so," said Kako amiably. She'd gone on to the knots of sash at Rafiq's chest. His struggling must have made them distinctly hard to untie, because it took her some time, tugging at the knots and wriggling the free ends, to loosen them.

"And what, I asked myself," continued Akish impressively; "Is the use of myriad sources of food, if we cannot eat of them?"

"Did you answer yourself?" Rafiq flicked a look up at Kako as she untied the last of his knots, and found that her eyes were laughing down at him.

Akish, unperturbed, said: "It was evident. The plants and fruits must have another use."

"And do they?"

"Each of them is an ingredient in a Door-opening spell between worlds. We can open a Door from here in Faery to the human world with the ingredients found here."

"Is that so?" murmured Kako. "Are you sure?"

For the first time, Prince Akish looked slightly uncomfortable. "All except for one: there isn't a petty-pink to be had in the garden."

"Never mind," Kako said soothingly. "It was a clever thought!"

"I say there aren't any in the garden because they're *outside* the garden!" said Prince Akish exasperatedly. "I can see them when I look over the wall."

"Well, it may as well be in one of the other Circles," said

Kako. "It's still Faery out there, and if you think we'll be able to get back in after being out there, I've got a horrible surprise for you."

"Perhaps not if we all went together," said the prince. "But if only one of us went? If one of us was harnessed to the others in the garden?"

Rafiq thought Kako sighed slightly as she untied the last of the knots that bound him to the tree. "That would probably work."

Akish, looking rather more satisfied that Rafiq liked to see him, nodded. "Very well. Rafiq–!"

"Don't bother to tell Rafiq," interrupted Kako. "He's part of your little rescue attempt and the Enchanted Keep will probably choose to consider he's taken a Door Out if he leaves the garden. I'm not part of the group, so if you tie the sashes around my waist and drop me over it should be safe enough."

There it was again, thought Rafiq. That unwillingness for either himself or Akish to climb over the wall and into Faery. Why was Kako so set against either of them venturing into Faery? He wished he'd thought to ask her that last night.

"The sashes aren't long enough," said Akish. "The petty-pinks are at least fifteen yards from the wall."

To Rafiq's eyes, Kako looked distinctly pale.

"Oh, at least," she agreed. "But the sashes will stretch just the same. Space in Faery is different when you're on a quest."

Prince Akish sniffed. "I've not heard any such thing."

Kako, busily tying one his sashes around her waist and draping the remaining sashes over one arm, said: "It's simple addition: one Enchanted Keep, one quest, and one required item, equals a warping in space and sometimes time."

The prince began to look distinctly annoyed, and Rafiq, to hide the grin he could feel spreading over his face, seized Kako by the elbows and carried her over to the closest wall.

Kako said: "How rude!" at him, and went back to knotting sashes. When she was finished she looped the other end around

Rafiq and tied it tightly around his waist, leaving a bare ten yards of sash between them.

"It won't be long enough," said the prince, sauntering toward them through the foliage.

Kako shrugged and said to Rafiq: "Boost me up, will you?"

Rafiq linked his fingers to make a stirrup, and when Kako put her bare foot in it he tossed her up on the wall.

"You'll have to come up here too," she said, treading lightly along the bricks. "Straddle the wall: one leg here, another there."

Rafiq did as he was told while Akish made remarks about the length of the sash-rope from below, and Kako knelt briefly before him.

"I don't know how long I'll be," she said: "And I'll probably disappear as soon as I hit the grass. Don't worry about that. Don't untie the sash for any reason, even if you think I'm not coming back. Don't believe everything you see. And be ready to haul me up again very quickly if I come on the run."

Rafiq, frowning, said: "Is it really that dangerous?" but Kako had already slithered down the other side of the wall, grasping his arm to let herself down lightly. Then she was gone.

Rafiq wasn't sure when he became aware of a small thought in the back of his mind that said Kako could break the spell that bound him to Akish. He was straddling the wall with one leg precariously in Faery and the other scarcely less precariously in the Enchanted Keep's domain, looking vainly to see Kako in the smooth greenery of Faery, and he could feel the bouncing tension in the line of sashes that told him she was still there. The thought came in so softly and quietly that he wasn't even sure of the veracity of it. He *was* sure, however, that she'd taken an interest in the spell; and he was even more sure that she knew far more about magic in general, and his spell in particular, than she pretended. Could she be persuaded to break it?

He was still pondering the point when there was a strangled shout from Akish.

"Look to the sky!" the prince yelled.

There was a bruising to it, a storm riding in; and in the centre of that storm was something big and bad and...toothy.

It was a basilisk. Rafiq gave it one horrified look and hauled desperately on the line of sashes, hand over hand.

"Cast the wench adrift!" shouted Akish. Rafiq heard the rattle of sword clearing scabbard as the prince took his stance in the garden below, and grimly braced himself to endure the pain of ignoring a Command. If he could hold out long enough, Kako would be back in the garden.

"Untie her and join me in the garden, you son of a lizard!" roared Akish. "Take your dragon form and prepare to fight!"

Rafiq reeled in the sashes, panting. He was certain that there was more sash than there should be, and still Kako was invisible–still the basilisk galloped furiously toward them. Then he felt a sudden tension in the line, a definite weight on the end, and heaved for dear life. The basilisk snarled its fury into his face, but Kako was in his arms with a wrenching thump, and they were falling backwards into the garden while the storm passed over their heads.

* * *

IN A CERTAIN LIBRARY somewhere in Shinpo, dissatisfaction was brewing.

"Where *is* she?" said Dai impatiently. "She said she'd come tonight!"

Zen shrugged. "Maybe they passed through another Circle. Stop pulling my hair, Dai!"

"Well, I've got to do *something*, and you're here."

"Stop pulling Zen's hair," said Suki wearily. "What's so dreadfully important, Dai?"

Dai shrugged, abandoning Zen's hair for more interesting

pursuits. "Kako asked us to do something for her. We did it and found out something she'll want to know."

"Something to do with Faery, I suppose?"

"Yes. Do you want to know about it?"

Suki said: "Not really, no. Is it dangerous?"

"Oh, *very!*" purred Dai. "Well. It is for the Fae, anyway."

The Fourth Circle is ended.

6

THE FIFTH CIRCLE

*R*afiq fell with Kako caught up in his arms. Instead of hitting grass, they hit stone, Kako's forehead cracking painfully against his chin as he tasted fiery blood. He cupped her head automatically as he sat up, murmuring his apologies into her hair.

Kako groaned miserably, but said: "Why are you sorry? I hit *you.*"

Rafiq laughed and spat blood. "I've had rougher landings. Was that a real basilisk?"

"Ah, so that's what I appeared as!" said Kako, her face lighting up. The motion of her face evidently caused her to feel the quickly swelling lump above her right eyebrow, and she winced. Rafiq ran his eyes over it, grinning.

"That bad, is it?" said Kako, untying the sashes that bound her to him. "Never mind, I can feel it. No, it wasn't a real basilisk: it was Faery playing tricks with you to see if you'd judge by appearance instead of knowledge. Or maybe it wanted to see if I trusted you. Who knows? You're bleeding."

Rafiq shrugged and lifted her with him as he rose, absently wiping his bleeding lip against his sleeve.

"Inside again," he said, flicking a glance up at the rough-hewn walls around them. This interior was subtly different from the usual interior of the Enchanted Keep, from the closely curving walls to the slits that cut slivers of daylight through the stonework. This was a real keep, one that didn't have the advantage of being enchanted. Whoever lived here had to physically fight off their enemies with arrows, slings and spears.

Kako was turning in a thoughtful circle, her gaze fluttering over the sparse room. "Where's the prince, I wonder?"

"He can't be far away," said Rafiq. "I'd know it if he was."

"Perhaps not," said Kako. She was prowling around the room, examining the furnishings. It was a small common-room with three doors leading from it and a few low, backless settees arranged around a large fireplace. "What sort of range can you get from the spell?"

"Three miles or so," he said.

"I thought so," Kako said, sounding pleased. "Well, the Keep must be interfering. You're more than three miles from the prince every time you come back home with me."

"You're lying to me," Rafiq said experimentally.

Kako's eyes widened very slightly. "Excuse me?"

"You're lying to me," he repeated, more sure of himself.

"Oh." Kako appeared to think about this. Then she asked: "About what?"

"What?"

"What am I lying about?"

"I don't know," said Rafiq, refusing to back down. "But I know you're lying."

"Well, that's just rude," said Kako, but her eyes were glowing with amusement. "If it makes you feel better, I'm not *technically* lying to you."

"It doesn't make me feel better."

Kako's shoulder slid up and down in that familiar half-shrug. "I have my moments of guilt. Oh, look! There's the prince."

"We'll discuss this later," growled Rafiq, as Prince Akish began tremulously to appear in the room.

At first they could see right through the prince, but by and by Akish grew more solid, though he didn't seem to be aware of his surroundings. In fact, he almost seemed...frozen. His sword was still drawn and in his hand, and he was still in the same fighting stance he'd taken when Kako tumbled back over the wall in Rafiq's arms.

When the prince had completely solidified there was a tiny magical *snap!* and Prince Akish looked around swiftly, his eyes wild. "What happened?"

"We finished the Fourth Circle," said Kako. "Well, actually, Rafiq finished it. Now we're in the Fifth, and you almost didn't make it."

"Whatever it was, it was intensely unpleasant," said the prince. "Don't do it again."

"There's a fine thank you!" Kako said indignantly. "Rafiq was the one who broke the Circle, after all. You were going to let me be slaughtered!"

"The Keep was testing to see if we'd trust our eyes or ourselves," Rafiq said, at Akish's enquiring look. "If we're now being tested on worth instead of puzzle solving–"

Akish slid his sword back into its scabbard and said testily: "I fail to see why you're concerned. She's only a servant, but I'm a prince and you're a dragon. Between us we've got enough nobility to pass any amount of tests of character."

"I'm sure you're right," said Kako in a soothing manner. "With such superior gentility we're sure to breeze right through these character-type Circles. I'm just lucky to be with you, aren't I?"

The prince gave her a hard look, but just as Rafiq thought he might be on the point of seizing Kako by the throat once again, there was a knock at the door.

"Lovely!" said Kako, darting to open it. "It's beginning!"

"My lords, my lady," said the man at the door. He was young and thin, with a slightly harried look that Rafiq instantly associated with a sheep well aware of its function as dinner and rather worried about the whole thing. "Welcome to Hawthorne Keep. We're so pleased that you've agreed to help us. Would you like a tour of the keep?"

"What is this nonsense?" said Akish, eyeing the man unfavourably.

"I'm almost certain we're in a Constructed environment," said Kako, surprising Rafiq with her openness. "All of this– none of it's real."

Both Akish and Rafiq turned a mistrustful look on her: Akish possibly because he didn't believe her, and Rafiq because it was highly suspicious of Kako to be so suddenly helpful. He wondered what that unusual honesty was in aid of.

Prince Akish said: "Why do you say that?"

"And what about him?" Rafiq asked, indicating the young man. He was waiting patiently for the three of them to finish talking, his face as worried as ever but somehow nothing more than slightly worried. Where was his confusion at their response– or his irritation at their rudeness for talking about him as though he wasn't there, for that matter?

"He's a Construct, too," Kako said. "And just have a look at the chairs, your highness. Look really closely. This settee has an ink stain at the front right-hand corner and a loose staple in the upholstering at the side."

"Bad workmanship and careless guests," shrugged Akish.

"Well, yes," admitted Kako; "But now look at the settee over by the wall."

"Look at the settee, Rafiq."

Rafiq, with another wondering look at the man who simply stood and waited for them, crossed the room to examine the settee. It had an ink stain in the front right-hand corner where the material pinched in, and a loose staple at the side just as Kako had described. Frowning, Rafiq checked the third settee. It was exactly the same.

"They're all copies," said Kako. "The Keep copied them all from one original. I'd lay odds on the fact that every settee around this Construct looks exactly like these three."

Prince Akish's eyes were narrow and thoughtful. "In that case, what does the vassal want?"

"I don't know," said Kako, shrugging. "Ask him."

"What do you want, vassal?"

The young man, as though released from a spell of silent politeness, said: "I'm here to welcome your honours to Hawthorne Keep. Would you like to be shown directly to the War Room, or would you like to be shown the extent of the keep and a view of the opposing army?"

Prince Akish turned a steely-eyed look on Kako. "He speaks as an ordinary vassal. The Keep has evidently confused his mind, but he's human enough."

"You think so?" said Kako, her eyes bright with challenge. "Ask him about the opposing army."

"Who is this opposing army?" demanded Akish.

The man, looking slightly less worried, hurried into speech: "The opposing army is the horde of the Arphadians, your honour. They covet our land with its rich pasture and plenteous waterways, and for many years now they've been encroaching upon our borders. Now at last they've launched a full attack, and outnumbered as we are, we've no certainty of deliverance unless your honours can–"

It was at this point that Kako grabbed him by the ears and kissed him full on the mouth, startling an exclamation from Prince Akish and a slight, fiery choke from Rafiq. The young man neither accepted nor repulsed the embrace, and when Kako released him and stepped back, he merely continued to speak as though he'd never been interrupted.

"–help us. Hawthorne Keep will hold for a few days, but we've not enough food to hold out for much longer and the Arphadians are desperately cunning."

Rafiq wasn't entirely certain as to the reactions that human courtship was supposed to evoke, but he was rather certain that if Kako had been kissing *him*, his reaction would have been very different.

She said: "See? The Keep didn't program him for romance. He's only programmed for interactions that are supposed to occur during the Story."

"Very well, I concede," said the prince. "We'll continue with the Story: no doubt if we rescue the people from their enemies it will send us through to the sixth Circle. The Keep is testing our courage."

An hour, one lengthy tour, and one short flight later, Rafiq had a very good idea of what was going on. The whole of Hawthorne Keep was one giant story construct into which the Enchanted Keep had deposited the three of them as somewhat dubious heroes, players in a game that seemed to hinge upon whether or not they could save Hawthorne Keep from the army at present encamped outside it.

Or at least, he thought, frowning, that's what Kako had suggested and the Prince seemed to believe. Knowing Kako a little better than he had in the beginning, he was highly suspicious of her helpfulness: moreover, he was just as mistrustful of the idea that the Enchanted Keep was testing their courage. The last Circle had tested something far more nebulous: that it was testing something so obvious as courage seemed unlikely.

The prince, however, was right in his element, planning and strategizing with the inmates of Hawthorne Keep. Rafiq, after reporting back from his flight to survey the Arphadians—a curiously spiky race of humanoid creatures that surrounded the keep like so many ants around a sugar lump—sat on one of the copied couches with Kako and watched Akish giving orders.

"He's very good at this, isn't he?" Kako said, in a congratulatory tone of voice. "Knows exactly what he's doing, how to use a fortress to the best advantage– I'm learning an awful lot."

Rafiq gazed down at her for long enough to make her eyes narrow slightly with amusement.

"What? You're not going to say I'm lying again, are you? I'm not."

"No," he said. "But you're like a fledgling in the sun, warm and complacent."

"Oh, you think I'm up to something!"

"No. I think finishing the story triumphant isn't what will take us to the next Circle."

Kako thought for a moment, and then said: "That depends on what you mean by triumphant."

"Is it what Akish would think of as triumphant?"

"I doubt it," she said, and offered him the plate of fruit she had been steadily decimating. If there was one thing Rafiq appreciated about this Circle, it was the sheer abundance, realness, and non-Faery quality of the food to be had. Even fresh fruit, which he would have scorned in his dragon form, was delightful to his human body. "It's fun to watch him try, though, isn't it?"

And it *was* fun to watch him try. It was also convenient, since when Akish joined in war-talks he tended to talk through the night and forget everything else, including Rafiq.

Rafiq left the room once the candles began to gutter and the fire was low, in search of warmth and perhaps a bed. A helpful servant was nearby to show him back to the common-room they'd arrived in that morning, and he was ushered through one of the doors around the room. It proved to be a spacious bedroom with its own fire, smaller than the one in the common-room but just as cheerful: no doubt Kako had been given one of the others that led from the common-room. That was, Rafiq thought, if she was still in Hawthorne Keep. Kako had slipped away from the war-talks earlier than he had, and she *had* stayed with him all last night when her family was expecting her back.

She was probably already in that warm, pleasant library talking secrets with Dai and Zen. He tried to ignore the flat edge of disappointment that pressed down on him at the thought and stretched out rather listlessly on the beautifully made bed. After all, what exactly had he expected? That she would come to fetch him? He might have lain there all night feeling sorry for himself if the door to his room hadn't snicked softly open an hour or so after he closed his eyes in a vain attempt to sleep.

Rafiq knew her footsteps, light and quick, and found himself smiling.

"I know you're awake," Kako said, bouncing down on his unused pillows. "Are you coming?"

"That depends," said Rafiq, rolling to face her. "Will there be more food?"

It was harder to get into the library that night. It was almost as though something was dragging at Rafiq's limbs as he walked; but it wasn't until they reached the library and Kako said: "What on *earth* have you done to my entrance?" that he knew it hadn't just been his imagination.

"Oh, *that*," said Dai. "That's because of all the fae who've sneaked in lately."

"Fae in the c– house? Why haven't I heard about it? Why didn't you tell me?"

Dai looked slightly guilty. "Akira didn't want to worry you. She said you were already busy trying to find a way to stop the fae."

"I *was*," said Kako, with a sideways look at Rafiq. "Then a prince and his murderous dragon attacked me. I was distracted."

"I didn't want to kill you," said Rafiq stiffly. "I had no choice. I don't make a habit of murdering females."

"You've hurt his feelings, now," Zen said. He was stretched out on his back on the couch closest to the fireplace, his ankles crossed and his nose ostensibly in a book.

Much to Rafiq's surprise, there was a flicker of amusement in the boy's eyes. That made him look more narrowly at Kako; and having looked, to realise that she was laughing at him.

"I'll be scarred for the rest of my life," Kako said sadly, but he wasn't fooled this time.

"I didn't get a very long look at the scar," he said. "How can I be sure I was the one who inflicted it? Show me again."

"*Kako!*" said three scandalised voices together. As Rafiq softly closed the gap between himself and Kako, Suki's voice won out to say in a squeak: "Has he seen your *neck? Kako*, you'll have to marry him now!"

"No, I won't!" spluttered Kako, slapping Rafiq's hands away from her scarf. "He didn't know it was against custom. Stop it, Rafiq! You're corrupting young minds!"

"*I* don't mind," said Dai, ignoring Zen's mutter of: "Of *course* you don't!"

Miyoko said, indignantly: "Raf has to marry me, not Kako!"

"This is beside the point," Kako said firmly: "Look, I closed the tear. How are the fae getting into Shinpo, let alone in here?"

"Some of 'em are coming through Llassar, some through Illisr," said Dai. "And dad thinks that some of 'em are coming through new Doors right here in Shinpo."

"I thought I had more time," said Kako ruefully. "Zen, did you do what I needed?"

"That? Oh yes, that was easy."

"What was easy?" demanded Rafiq. As disappointing as it was that his previous gambit had been overturned, the conversation had become distinctly interesting. Zen looked torn: he'd obviously done something he was quite proud of despite his dismissive attitude, and he looked as though he would very much like to share his cleverness.

At last, however, he said: "Oh, nothing in particular."

"Sit down and have a cup of tea," said Dai. "Later on we'll talk about that thing you wanted me to look at. You're going to like what I discovered."

Since it was obvious that they weren't going to discuss whatever it was they were so jubilantly hinting about in front of him,
Rafiq heeded the small tuggings of Miyoko upon his cuffs, and
allowed himself to be pulled to the opposite end of the room.

"Sit," said Miyoko, pointing at the hearth. Rafiq, much
amused, sat. She sat down opposite him with her legs crossed and
her stomach poking out, and looked expectantly at him.

Rafiq said: "What?"

"Burn it," Miyoko said, as if to an imbecile, and he saw that
she'd heaped dust bunnies and twists of paper in the otherwise
empty hearth.

"No," said Rafiq.

Miyoko whined: "But *Rafiq*..."

"Kako will scold me."

She regarded him for a silent moment, then said with great
craftiness: "Kako won't scold. Dragons are *supposed* to burn."

"I'm not a dragon. I'm a man."

"Oh," she said sorrowfully. And then, more cheerfully:
"Matches? Magic?"

"No," said Rafiq, his eyes on Kako. Dai had very carefully
passed her something that was wrapped in a handkerchief, and
Kako's eyes were shining with more animation than he'd ever
seen from her. "Why is Kako happy?"

"Presents," said Miyoko, shrugging. "Kako likes presents."

Kako had brought something with her last time she visited
her family. Something from the Keep, wondered Rafiq, or something she got from elsewhere– Prince Akish, for instance? If so,
why? What could Akish have that was worth stealing to Kako?
And when had she done it? He thought about it until she put the
folded handkerchief in her pocket, and until Dai left the room,
looking pleased.

Then he trod lightly up behind Kako and said in her ear: "It
was a very good performance. I thought the faint was real."

Kako jumped and made a stifled noise, which made him grin.

"The faint was real," she said, when her breathing became even again. "He was crushing my windpipe. Very uncomfortable."

"Then why needle him into attacking you?"

"I needed to get him a lot closer than he'd normally allow himself to be to a maid," Kako said, surprising him by being absolutely honest. "I can't pick pockets from a distance. Are you choking? You'd better sit down."

"So you did pick his pocket!"

"Yes. You really should sit down. You look a little strange."

Rafiq laughed aloud and sat down. He'd thought when he met Kako as a dragon that she was as deadly as she was small. It was surprising to realise that Kako in her human form was even more deadly than Kako in her dragon form. "What did you take from him?"

"Something that wasn't his. It's not mine either, but it's probably safer with me until the proper owner comes for it."

"You're not going to tell me."

He thought that Kako looked regretful. "No. Sorry."

"You're not supposed to tell him you're hiding things from him," said Dai, returning to the room. Behind her was a short, pleasant-faced woman with an elaborately coiffed head of hair but no head-dress or neck scarf. Kako's mother, Rafiq realised, with a stab of dismay. He leapt to his feet as Kako rose gladly to embrace the woman.

"I didn't mean to interrupt you," she said remorsefully.

"You didn't, my little clever one," said the woman, hugging her tightly. "The day is done and we've all gone home."

Dai said: "I thought *I* was your little clever one!"

"You're my slightly smaller clever one," said Kako's mother. "Am I to be introduced to the dragon, my dears?"

"Mother, this is Rafiq," Kako said. "Rafiq, this is my mother."

Rafiq found himself bowing, which was something of a surprise. It was polite to bow to a woman, of course; but he'd worked with Akish long enough to know not to bow to servants.

"It's a pleasure to meet you," said Kako's mother, inclining her head in return. "We *were* expecting you last night, you know."

"We had a bit of trouble with some fae water," said Kako. "Rafiq was trying to climb over a wall into Faery and I had to tie him up."

"She tied me to a chair once," said Dai. "What'd she tie you to?"

"A tree," said Rafiq. "Why did she tie you up?"

"Fae plum. We were experimenting. Fae things pack a bit of a wallop, don't they?"

"Yes," Rafiq said briefly.

"Children, why don't you talk amongst yourselves," said Kako's mother. "Rafiq and I wish to speak together for a moment."

Kako, looking rather startled, said: "Mama–!"

"I have some questions for him," said the lady, and though her voice was as pleasant as ever, Kako melted into the group of siblings without another word. It surprised and rather worried Rafiq, who watched her go with a feeling akin to abandonment. Dai allowed herself to be subsumed by the group as well, twitching a rueful and sympathetic brow at him, and Rafiq was left to the gentle smile of their mother.

HAWTHORNE KEEP BECAME ABRUPTLY MORE serious the next day, when Rafiq made his first airborne attack under Akish's orders. Neither had quite acknowledged the fact, but Rafiq thought they must have both expected the weapons of the spiky humanoids below to be as unreal as the Constructed story. When Rafiq swept low and swift over the army to lay down a blistering stream of fire, such a hail of arrows and spears hissed at him that he banked automatically: and in so doing possibly saved his own life. As it was, one of the spears tore through his right wing, slitting the stretched skin there and tossing him into a dangerous sideslip that ended heavily and painfully on the tower from which he'd begun.

Kako, who had somehow managed to be one of the tower party, darted around the other humans and ducked beneath Rafiq's awkwardly stiff wing to run her hands over the tear. He felt the snarl of pain rising through his stomach, mixed with fire, and fought back the urge to snap at her.

"It's not too dreadful," she said. "But you should change to human again. Trust me. It'll help."

Akish said: "Hmm. I did not expect their weapons to hurt us. Nor did I expect them to be immune to your dragonfire: not a one of them dropped! Wench, what is the meaning of this?"

For once, Kako seemed to be entirely taken aback. "I didn't– I wasn't– I don't know. I really don't know. I didn't expect this at all."

Rafiq changed slowly and painfully until he was somewhat familiarly human again, and said: "Taking your revenge, were you?"

"Don't be a baby," said Kako, though her face was still pale. "You're not even injured anymore."

Rafiq looked incredulously down at his arm, and instead of a bloody gash he saw a new scar. His eyes met Kako's, his mouth working to form the right words; words that wouldn't inadvertently betray her to Akish. At last, he simply said: "How?"

Kako shrugged her shoulder. "I don't know for sure. My theory is that the physical change from dragon to human rewrites the whole of your body every time."

"Why the scar, then?" asked Rafiq, unconsciously flexing the muscle.

"I don't know that for sure, either. I think it's because the magic doesn't know exactly what to do with it. It's like a grain of grit in the workings: it doesn't stop the workings, but it makes them move just a little jerkily. The scar is a flaw in the construct."

"We'll have to change our plans," said Akish, without heeding either Rafiq or Kako. "A close aerial assault is obviously out of the question. If this constructed environment allows us to be injured or killed, all my assumptions will have to be reassessed. Back to the war room!" He made for the tower stairs in an energetic swirl of cloak and sword, followed by an eager trail of armoured men and women.

Kako, closely observing the new scar on Rafiq's arm, said: "Do you think he wants us down there too?"

"Probably," said Rafiq. He was disinclined to move. The sunshine was pleasantly warm, Kako's curious fingers were not unpleasantly running over his new scar, and he had never felt either more human, or more content to be so.

A warm summer breeze picked up, wafting over the turrets and confusing Rafiq with its sense of oddity until he realised why it was so alien. "There's no smell here," he said.

"Yes, I noticed that," murmured Kako, prodding at his scar. "It's a bit off-putting, isn't it? I don't think the Keep knows about scent. Rafiq?"

"Mmm?"

"What did my mother ask you yesterday?"

Too late, Rafiq found that he'd stiffened. No use pretending *now* that Kako's mother had simply wished to become better acquainted with him.

"She asked me what I'd do once you broke my Thrall to the Illisran Crown."

The question had taken him by surprise at the time, and he had answered with the absolute truth: he would stay at the Enchanted Keep with Kako, of course. As the thought blossomed, it had seemed natural. Both Kako and the princess would benefit from the addition of another dragon, and it had occurred to Rafiq at much the same time that he would also benefit from the addition of another dragon. From there, perhaps it would be possible to convince Kako of the benefits of having another human in the Keep, too.

Kako's eyes were very wide: whatever she'd expected him to say, it hadn't been that. *"Really?"*

"Mmm. She said you had some ideas about how to do it." She had also, very gently and in no uncertain terms, made Rafiq aware that Kako's family could and *would* slowly take him apart piece by quivering piece if he so much as looked at her in the wrong way. Since relating that particular part of the conversation would have taken *this* conversation in a way that Rafiq wasn't yet prepared for it to go, he thought it best not to mention it.

Thus, when Kako looked enquiringly at him and demanded: "What else?" he merely shrugged.

Her eyes narrowed very slightly, but she seemed to accept that. She tipped her head toward the tower stairs and asked: "Is he likely to come up with a good plan?"

Rafiq considered this. With Akish involved, the merit or otherwise of the plan would depend entirely upon who you happened to be and how important the prince believed you to be. For Akish, the plan would undoubtedly turn out to be good: the prince had a way of looking after himself that was tantamount to genius. For Rafiq, it was also likely to turn out well, but not absolutely guaranteed: Akish was unlikely to want to see him dead or injured, but if it was a choice between himself or Rafiq, Rafiq knew who would come out safely. When it came to Kako, things were very much shakier.

Of one thing, Rafiq was very certain. If, as seemed increasingly possible, they *could* die in this construct, it was entirely likely that they *would* die, be the prince never so crafty. The Arphadians were far too many for the people of Hawthorne Keep, and if dragonfire had no effect on them, it was unlikely that the keep would last many more nights. He couldn't even fly away if Akish didn't order it, since leaving the prince there would be tantamount to causing his death, and he was Burdened not to do so.

Kako, seeing his struggles, gave a little spurt of laughter and said: "Oh, never mind! I suppose that makes it clear, after all. We should have an interesting night."

Night came and brought with it darkness, confusion, and a sudden change in circumstances. Rafiq woke to a sickening feeling that everything was double—or perhaps even triple—and was prevented from emptying the contents of his stomach on his bedroom floor only by the merciful return of coherence to his sight. By then that single-sight was showing him the rapid influx of spikily armed men to his bedchamber, and a shouting from Akish's bedroom informed him that the prince had been similarly overcome. Rafiq dived for the door in an instant, narrowly avoiding two wickedly sharp knives that sliced at him in passing, and was halfway to Kako's bedroom before it occurred to him to wonder why his Burden hadn't forced him to go to Prince Akish's aid instead. The thought flitted in and out again immediately, because he was then so busy fighting to get to Kako's side that he had no room for any other thought. At the entrance of the Arphadians—for it could only be the Arphadians—she had been awake quickly enough to rapidly scale the frame of her canopied bed, from which vantage point she was at present hailing sharp, deadly spells down on the company.

Rafiq, having tried and failed to change into his dragon form, had no time to dwell upon the somewhat terrifying fact. Instead, he wrestled a knife from a bulky Arphadian who didn't stand up well to a solid blow to the base of the skull, and furiously slashed with it, edging his way toward Kako and the bed. He had only a rudimentary idea of hand to hand fighting, however, and his wildness notwithstanding, the result was a foregone conclusion. Rafiq was borne to the floor not two yards away from the foot of the bed, painfully beset by Arphadian boots and fists.

Curling into a defensive ball with his head ringing from the kicks, he heard one of the Arphadians say: "For the last time, will you come down!"

"Oh, all right, all *right!*" Kako said disgustedly. "Look, stop kicking him! I'm coming down!"

The leading Arphadian gave Rafiq one more kick for good measure, then casually tore Kako from the curtains as she climbed down. She fell heavily, and without a sound but the crack of her head against stone as she hit the floor. Rafiq spat blood and tried to crawl toward her, but he was dragged from the room and Kako alike by one leg, jolting over the stone floor until he was in the common-room again. Akish was being shoved through the door of his own bedroom; furious, dishevelled, and disarmed.

"Change, you maggoty son of a lizard!" he howled.

"Can't!" croaked Rafiq, aware of two missing teeth and a possibly torn tongue. "The Keep is preventing me."

"You're a good fighter," said the Arphadian leader to Rafiq. "That one is, too, but he had the advantage of cold steel. I think you want to live."

"Do you?" said Rafiq in cold rage, thinking of Kako lying senseless and perhaps dead in her bedroom.

"I do, my bucko, I do."

Rafiq gave him a narrow look that was made all the narrower because his left eye was rapidly swelling shut. "What if I do?"

"Well now, if I was to be convinced that you'd turned— become part of the Arphadian army—I'd be inclined to save your life."

"Convinced, how?" asked Rafiq, his thoughts flying very quickly. Was there a chance of getting Kako out of this alive?

The Arphadian grinned. "Oh, you'd have to be obedient. *Very* obedient. And you'd have to cut all ties to your past."

"Cut ties," said Rafiq slowly, because it sounded as though the man had used the words deliberately. The Arphadian was turning a dagger in one hand, rolling it lightly from finger to finger, and when Rafiq's eyes rose from the dagger to his eyes, the man jerked his head in Akish's direction.

"Kill your companions," he said, this time plainly and clearly. "Earn our trust, and at the same time destroy any chance of being accepted by your countrymen again. Of course, it's unlikely any of them will live through the night, but the chance, my friend, the chance!"

"You will not kill me!" shouted Akish. "I Burden you!"

Rafiq waited for the Burden to settle on him, heavy and impossible to ignore, but it never fell. He drew a slow breath, his thoughts whirring away madly, and came to the conclusion that the Keep was preventing his Thrall from being used against him. He could kill Akish here and now, without the Burden stopping him.

Kako, on the other hand, he certainly couldn't kill. "I won't kill the girl," he said. "Keep her safe and I'll do whatever you want."

"The girl's dead already," said the captain. His lips were still moving, and he might have said something like: "Just him then. Do you want to live, or not?" but Rafiq's hearing had gone distinctly fuzzy.

The Arphadians laughed when he staggered to his feet, a scattering of half-respectful, half-derisive mirth. Rafiq's thoughts were as fuzzy as his hearing: it seemed to him that if he had neither knife nor dragonfire to kill the man who had killed Kako, he would tear out his throat with his teeth. He snarled and leapt for the captain, and in leaping he flew through dark and cold and the last of the Fifth Circle...

* * *

SOMEWHERE IN THE depths of the Fifth Circle a pair of legs protruding from one of Hawthorne Keep's walls kicked disconsolately. Prince Akish's legs—for they were his—seemed to have intended to follow the rest of his body through the gelatinous wall but hadn't quite made it. The legs kicked once, twice more, while a ripple surged slowly and impressively across the reality of the wall as it became slightly less than real. One more surge, another kick, and the legs were dragged unceremoniously into the Sixth Circle.

The Fifth Circle is ended.

7

THE SIXTH CIRCLE

*R*afiq was plunged into brackish water before his stomach had time to catch up with him. It closed over his head in a rush, sparking a white hot panic that made him flail wildly with his arms and legs, clawing at insubstantial water. Then something gripped the back of his shirt and hoisted him upward, and Rafiq felt his head break the surface. He beat uselessly at the water, casting about desperately for anything solid to cling to, his eyes wide and frozen.

"Stop it, Rafiq!" hissed a voice in his ear.

Rafiq heard it as from a distance in his mad, thrashing panic. It wasn't until something painful pierced his ear that he was shocked into the realisation that it was Kako's voice in his ear. She wasn't dead or injured. She wasn't still lying in the fifth Circle with a pool of blood spreading from her cracked head. She was here with him, her arms around him from behind to keep his head above water. It was she who had dragged his head above water, she who had–

"You *bit* my *ear!*"

"Didn't have a hand free to slap you," panted Kako. "Anyone would think you hadn't had to swim before."

"Haven't," said Rafiq shortly, grimly concentrating on *not* windmilling madly with his arms. It didn't feel like it, but he knew Kako was keeping him afloat with her arms around his chest and the slow, steady stroke of her legs.

"I'm going to put you over by the wall," she said. "It'll give you something to hold onto. Try not to kick me again, won't you?"

"Again?"

"And if you hit me again I'll bite your other ear."

"I *hit* you?"

"Well, it was more of a glancing blow," said Kako. "But it's probably going to bruise. There you go."

It took Rafiq several waterlogged seconds to realise that she was nudging him into a curving wall of slimy brick. He seized upon two of them that protruded sufficiently to offer grip and threw a glazed look around. They were in a well, the opening a bright circle of light far above, and the walls curving around them in serried ranks that rose higher than Rafiq could easily follow until they met the opening. Here and there one jutted out further than its fellows, a possible but not very probable route of escape. As far down as they were, the light was green and soft, and made the water seem almost yellow.

Kako, who was still supporting him with one hand and calmly stroking through the water with the other, said: "It's too deep to reach the bottom as well. I checked just before you fell through."

Rafiq tried not to let the idea of bottomless depth take hold on his mind. "What happened? Where's Akish?"

"What do you think happened?" Kako said disgustedly. "He killed us. The Keep is trying to keep him out of the sixth Circle because technically, he hasn't passed."

"We're alive," said Rafiq, his eyes catching an eruption of bubbles against the curve of the wall across from him. He ran his tongue over his teeth and found that they were all there again.

Kako managed to shrug in a silent ripple of stagnant water. "That doesn't mean he didn't kill us. The Keep likes to make things safe– well, until the last Circle, anyway. It split us into three separate Constructs: didn't you feel the split?"

"*That's* what that was?"

"The split vision? Yes. The Keep copied us and put a copy into each of the Constructs to interact with the others. The prince killed Constructs of us: the same deal that was offered to you."

Rafiq said: "You told us it was all a construct."

"Well, it was."

"Yes, but the only way through it was to pretend that it was real, and to act as we would have if it *was* real."

"Are you angry because I misled you, or because you forgot it wasn't real?"

"I'm not angry!" said Rafiq angrily. In truth, he was angry because it was hard to remember that Kako was alive, though he was speaking to her. The feelings that the fifth Circle had stirred up were still raging, high and fierce, somewhere deep inside him.

Kako said: "I see that," and smiled at him, warm and apologetic. The warmth of it utterly did away with his anger, but left him shivering in its wake with reaction or perhaps cold. He felt stiff and wrong and somehow extinguished in the wet embrace of the well.

"There's something over there," he said, his attention again caught by a burst of bubbles.

"Yes, it's probably Prince Akish drowning," sighed Kako. "Can you hold onto the wall for a bit?"

Rafiq, who desperately wanted to say no, said: "Yes," and Kako vanished beneath the yellow surface in a brief flurry of pink silk and bare feet. He watched the bubbling mass of air breaking the surface over by the wall with clenched teeth and the savage thought that he would much rather Akish drown alone and perhaps take with him all hope of breaking Rafiq's indenture to the crown, than that Kako should also drown in the rescuing of him.

She stayed beneath the water so long that the bubbles ceased to froth at the surface, and Rafiq began to think that she really had drowned. Then there was a shallow disturbance in the surface: a swirling indent that gave way to a slight bulge, and Kako slid silently into the green light once again. Close by her head bobbed another, and two limp arms floated to the surface as she towed Akish toward Rafiq. He wondered if he'd looked quite so pathetic when she did the same for him.

"Had to get his chainmail off," she said. "Can you hold the front of his gambeson? At the waist? His legs and arms will float by themselves."

Rafiq put out one stiff hand to grip a handful of Akish's gambeson, feeling distinctly perilous. "Is he dead?"

"No. Well, sort of. If I can force the water from his lungs he'll be fine."

Forcing the water from Prince Akish's lungs proved to be a short and violent business that almost jolted Rafiq from his handhold. Once she had the prince on his back, Kako proceeded to vigorously pump at his chest with the heel of one hand, the other supporting his shoulders. After the fourth or fifth assault Akish convulsed in the water, his chest jerking up to meet his knees, and regurgitated a disturbing amount of yellowish water.

Kako immediately rolled him to one side despite his feeble struggles, patting him encouragingly on the back, and when he stopped coughing and gasping Prince Akish seemed content to float with one hand on her shoulder. He was a swift and capable swimmer, Rafiq knew: he wondered exactly why the prince had almost drowned.

Kako, her eyes glowing with golden-brown mischief, met his eyes and said: "His legs were stuck over in the fifth Circle."

"Curse you, wench, do you never stop talking?" rasped Prince Akish.

"*There's* a fine thank you!" instantly said Kako. "Should I have let you drown?"

There was a brief silence before Akish said: "You were useful to me. Where is my chainmail?"

"It didn't float."

Rafiq saw the moment that a catastrophic idea struck the prince. There was a splashing as the prince's fingers frantically patted down the front of his gambeson where Rafiq knew he had a secret pocket, then a swirling of water as Akish's arms circled to keep himself afloat, relief etched clear in his face. Kako must have put back whatever it was she had stolen from him.

Implausibly oblivious, Kako said: "When you're rested, your highness, we might as well proceed to the next Circle."

Akish stared at her. "How? I thought only the princess and the dragon knew the way through the Circles?"

"When I was stripping you of your chainmail it slipped through my fingers and caught on something in the wall further down," said Kako. "And out of the water, further up, right *there*– that's a lever. I'd stake my scarf the chainmail caught on an underwater one. If you're not going to take the Door Out–"

"I'm not!"

"–then I suggest that one of us climbs to the top lever, another swims to the lower lever, and we pull them together."

Prince Akish thought about it for a long time, and at length voiced the same suspicion that Rafiq had been nursing. "You're unusually helpful, wench. Why?"

"Normally I'd try to stall you," Kako said, shrugging a circle of ripples. "But Rafiq doesn't like it here: so, on to the seventh Circle! It'd be much safer for you if you left now, though."

"I have prevailed until now," the prince said stiffly. "I shall prevail yet."

"You know, I think you really believe that. Your certainty is actually terrifying."

"Rafiq can dive for the underwater lever," Akish said, even more stiffly. "You'll climb for the one above water. I shall remain here."

"Rafiq can't swim."

"I'll climb for the top one," Rafiq said wearily. His shivers had become full, body-wracking shudders.

"Shaking like that? I don't think so. You'd just fall back in and I'd have to rescue you again. No, you'll have to stay here. I'll pull the top lever."

"How do I know you won't let me drown and take the Door Out?" said Akish immediately.

Rafiq grinned. He had expected nothing else.

"You don't," said Kako, cheerfully comfortless. "That's the point, you see?"

Akish gave her a hard look. "I do see. Nevertheless, between what the Keep intends and what its guests do, there is a wide chasm that makes me exceedingly uncomfortable."

"Well," said Kako. "What about Rafiq? Do you think he'd let you drown?"

"No," Akish said, his head jerking back in surprise. "He can't. The Burden laid upon him forbids him bringing about, being party to, or in any way encompassing my death. Besides, his slavery is to the crown in general as much as me in particular. If I die, he remains enslaved."

"*Well* then..." Kako said, shrugging. She was clinging close to the wall now, her sodden scarf wrapped so tightly around her neck that Rafiq was surprised she could breathe. As he watched, she made a clean, lithe lunge from the water and caught at one of the bricks higher up. For a moment she hung from her fingertips, perilously close to falling again, then another short burst of effort saw her other hand firmly in place on another brick and one foot in a hollow spot.

When Kako reached the ledge there was a scuffle and a slight shriek from above.

Rafiq, one hand reaching for the first brick in the climb up, said: "Kako! Are you all right?"

Her voice floated back down apologetically. "Sorry! There was a rat up here."

"You're afraid of rats?"

"It *surprised* me!" came the indignant reply.

Akish, with no patience for Rafiq's teasing, said: "Wench, do you have the lever?"

"Yes. How long will it take you to get to yours?"

"Give me a count of ten," said Akish. He was peering down into the water, where Rafiq thought he could see a faint glitter of silver: Akish's chainmail, no doubt. "It's not so far down, but I'll need time to position myself."

"Will you go now?"

A splash and a ripple answered her. At Rafiq's internal count of two, she said: "Rafiq?"

"Yes?"

"The water is going to sink. Probably quite rapidly. You'll need to keep holding onto the wall, because the current will be quite strong, but you'll need to keep changing your grip to follow it down."

With a feeling of dread, Rafiq said: "Yes," and began to feel below the water for his next hand-hold. As he did, there was the grinding of gears from above, accompanied by a shower of rust and cobwebs. A dimple appeared in the centre of the well, lazily spinning, and as lazily spread until it was a rippling coil fully to the edges of the well. Rafiq, already aware that he was sinking lower in the well and seeking another hand-hold, found that his legs were being slowly sucked away from the wall and tried to fight down his panic.

Kako's voice said from above: "Don't be startled, Rafiq; but it's going to get noisy soon."

Rafiq started to say: "Noisy?" but the word was muffled by an unearthly wail that rose in the close air of the well and tore at his eardrums. He desperately tried to cover his ears, but by then the pull of the spinning water was so strong that he needed both hands just to stay by the wall. If he had felt a sympathy approaching horror for Akish's part in this Circle, Rafiq now felt that the prince, in having his ears clogged with water, was the fortunate one. The wail was so painful, in fact, that when it stopped all Rafiq could think about was the blessed relief of the silence. It took the rapidly rising water and Kako's rather impolite remarks from her perch high above him to make him realise that something must have gone wrong.

Akish burst from the water shortly after that, spitting water and coughing.

"Curse you wench, you *were* trying to drown me!"

A barely audible mutter of: "Oh, for *pity's sake!*" floated down to them.

"Repeat yourself, wench!"

"I *said*, your highness, that the water needs *time to sink*! You're going to be under water for quite some time– longer if you keep letting go of your lever and have to fight the current to get back to the surface!"

Akish looked to Rafiq for confirmation. "The water was sinking," Rafiq said. "It was only a yard or two above your head."

"You must have been able to feel the current!" said Kako exasperatedly.

"Mind your tone, wench! I shall dive again."

There was another mutter from above them, but this time Rafiq couldn't make out any of the words. It was probably just as well. Akish evidently thought so as well, and since he couldn't reach her anyway, he merely snapped: "Begin your count!" and dived again.

This time Rafiq was prepared for the ear-splitting squeal and the drag of the water. It didn't make the experience any pleasanter, but it *did* make it possible for him to keep passing hand over hand in a steady, aching routine without panicking. He did that until Akish's head broke water again. This time the prince was still attached to his lever.

Apparently Kako placed little trust in his continuing to do so, because she shouted above the wail: "*Don't* let go! Don't let go until the water is completely gone!"

By the time all the water had disappeared, vanishing through a round hole at the base of the well, Rafiq was shivering on a slimy bed of something unpleasant and organic, Akish was still clinging to his lever just in sight, and Kako was entirely out of sight in the gloom, presumably still with her lever.

"Shall I release my hold?" bellowed Akish, and it wasn't until Rafiq heard a faint, garbled reply that he realised the prince was talking to Kako. She must have answered in the affirmative, because Akish began to carefully make his way down to the base of the well. The bricks were much slipperier as the bottom of the well drew nearer, and when the prince was still some way above Rafiq's head, the hand-holds ceased completely.

Akish snarled, shifting his already perilous grip. He'd flung his chainmail over his shoulder, and with the added weight of his water-logged gambeson and the strain of clinging with his fingertips, it was looking exceedingly likely that he would fall. He dropped the chainmail with a grunt and it made a soft, wet slap against the slick floor beside Rafiq.

"You'll have to slow my fall," said Akish. "To break a leg at this stage in the game is insupportable."

"The floor is slippery," Rafiq told him, but Akish had already released his grip. The prince caught at his shoulders, Rafiq at *his* forearms, and Akish sank to the knee in slick, green algae.

Akish made a sound of disgust and tugged at his feet. They emerged from the algae with a wet sucking sound, but barely had the holes begun to soften around the edges and fill with thick green water before Kako dropped from the darkness and made another pair.

"It's all a bit nasty, isn't it?" she said cheerfully, catching at Rafiq's elbow to prevent herself falling over. "The door is over there, I believe. Perhaps we should rest before we go through to the seventh Circle. I doubt we'll have a chance to rest when we get there."

"Why?" demanded Akish. "What is in the seventh Circle?"

"Not even the princess or the dragon know that," Kako said; and this time, Rafiq was certain that she spoke the exact truth. "The Keep has one or two secrets known only to itself."

"Very well, then: I see no use in waiting," said Prince Akish. "Onward, Rafiq! Onward, wench!"

Rafiq saw Kako take a deep breath in through her nose, and felt her fingers tighten in the crook of his arm. Her eyes met his; uncertain, uneasy, and slightly apologetic. Rafiq wasn't sure what his eyes told her, but whatever it was, it made her chin set suddenly. More pleasantly, it made her smile up at him; openly, honestly and cheerfully.

She said: "Shall we?"

They stepped into the seventh Circle together.

* * *

IN A GRAND, high-ceilinged room somewhere in the centre of Shinpo, a pleasant-faced woman attending a well-filled meeting of state suddenly went very pale and ceased to listen to the main speaker. She whispered briefly and urgently to the tall girl beside her and vanished from the room at a genteel trot, her exit hidden by several large, broad-shouldered men and one particularly deadly-sharp woman.

Once in the hall outside, she fairly ran, her elaborate head-dress wobbling dangerously, and arrived via a circuitous route of back allies and secret passages to a comfortable, well-lit library, where a slightly chubby gentleman caught her at the door and embraced her soothingly.

"Mama!" said Zen, surprised into the childish appellation. He was in his usual seat, but he wasn't reading.

"I thought you were–"

"I was. What happened?"

"The passage has vanished," said Dai, biting her thumb. "It was just here, and now it's gone."

"Did Kako do it, or was it the Keep itself?"

"The Keep," said Suki worriedly. "It's closed up completely."

"Where is Kako?"

Dai looked away. "We think she's in the seventh Circle."

"Is the dragon with her?" asked the plump gentleman.

"Of course he is, dear," said Kako's mother.

"Probably," said Zen at the same time. "She's got the shard, after all."

"Will that be enough to keep him near her?"

Kako's mother smiled, as if involuntarily. "That, amongst other things."

Kako's father said: "*Other* things? What other things? What have I missed?"

Dai laughed suddenly. "Never you mind, Father! Do you think you can open another passage?"

"Not a chance," he said. "How Kako did it in the first place, I haven't a clue. We'll have to wait until it opens again."

Miyoko, her lower lip sticking out, sat down by the curtains that had once contained a passage to the Enchanted Keep but now hid only solid brick. Zen, after a moment's indecision, did the same. Dai, sighing, dragged a chair closer and threw herself into it, and Suki leant gracefully against the wall. Kako's mother slid her arms around her husband's waist in return, allowed her head to sink on his shoulder...and they waited.

The Sixth Circle is ended.

8

THE SEVENTH CIRCLE

*P*rince Akish looked almost unbearably self-satisfied. Rafiq didn't think he'd ever wanted to hit the man so much in all his life. The thought worried him a little. His more violent thoughts had always been distinctly dragonish, whether he was in human or dragon form: this was the first time his impulses had been human.

He felt Kako's fingers in the crook of his elbow, and was reminded that perhaps it wasn't exactly the *first* time his impulses had been entirely human. He smiled down at her, but Kako wasn't looking at him. She was gazing around the room with a particularly blank face. That also troubled him slightly, since Kako with a blank face was a worried Kako. He followed her eyes around the room and discovered exactly what it was that was worrying her: there was no Door Out. She had said as much in one of the earlier Circles, but Rafiq hadn't realised exactly how trapped that would make him feel. Prince Akish must not have noticed, because his smugness only seemed to expand.

"What is the manner of this challenge?" the prince demanded. "Wench! Cease your goggling! What is the manner of this challenge?"

"I don't know," Kako said, her hand slipping away from Rafiq's arm. Against the brilliant white of the room her algae-soiled trousers looked even dirtier, and her cobweb-frosted head-dress looked particularly shabby.

"I've told you in every Circle so far that the seventh is unknown except to the Keep. I have no help to give you, and there's no Door Out. You're on your own."

Prince Akish's eyes seemed to glow with feverish excitement. "Very well! One last challenge! I shall be equal to it!"

All three of them gazed around in silence. It was a vast white room: white tiled floor, white walls, white ceiling. There were no windows and no doors—not even the one by which they had ostensibly entered—and the walls were all of a uniform height and length. The only difference to the walls was in the one directly opposite them, which had a wide, deep alcove in it. It was well lit, and bare except for a low, round piece of furniture that could have been a small footstool but didn't quite seem to be.

The prince was already striding forward to examine it, and when he dropped to one knee to run his fingers over the surface of it there was silence for a good few moments.

Then he said: "Lizard. Look at this."

Rafiq, strangely reluctant to approach the thing, did as he was told. There were criss-crossing straight lines chipped into the footstool, or low table—whatever it was—deep, certain, and vicious.

"That must have taken a bit of effort," said Kako, who had wandered along behind them. She slipped between the two of them and crouched to examine it. "It's marble too, isn't it?"

"Indeed," said Prince Akish. "Most curious. We will examine the room."

"I don't think there's much to examine," Kako said.

Rafiq had to agree. But for the alcove, there wasn't anything to be seen. He walked around the room anyway, one hand trailing along the wall with the hopeful suspicion that a trick of the light hid a passage out in all the white that surrounded them. He found nothing: the walls were simply walls, the corners were corners, and the floor proved only to be the same marble tile as the rest of the Keep.

Akish was tapping at the tiles with his sabatons—checking for hollowed out tiles?—and Kako, who seemed to be doing something very strongly magical with one hand, very carefully walked so as to keep what she was doing hidden from the others. She was so very careful about it, in fact, that Rafiq began to wonder if she knew the way out of the seventh Circle too.

He considered the idea, observing Kako in his peripheral, but ultimately dismissed it. She had been genuinely concerned about entering the seventh Circle, unlike the other Circles. She had obviously been convinced that it was dangerous, and had done everything she could to convince Prince Akish to take a Door Out before they got to it. She had been very clear, moreover, about the fact that she didn't know how to complete the seventh Circle. Rafiq didn't think she'd been lying: he'd begun to know her quite well, and though she might have some idea of what needed to be done *now*, he was certain she hadn't known when they entered the room. Still, it seemed like a sensible idea to keep his eye on her.

It was fortunate that Kako happened to be on the alcove side of the room when something red and shiny began to appear beside the round marble block. It meant that Rafiq, who was still watching her, had a reasonably good view of what happened. It happened very quickly: a slight gleam of metallic red to the air beside the marble block that clanked in a horribly familiar way.

"Who goes there!" said Akish at once, wheeling toward Kako and the disturbance.

Kako gave a muffled squeak and sprang away from the impending threat, her magic-entwined hand flashing forward defensively. By then the red glint had become a tall, visored knight in shiny red armour, whose plumed helmet was only dwarfed by the battle-axe he carried.

Akish stared up at the strapping knight. "What in the–!"

Kako, putting her hand back into her pocket, said thoughtfully: "That looks awfully sharp, doesn't it?" Her eyes were flitting from the axe to the block, and Rafiq, who had seen his fair share of beheadings, felt a creeping sense of foreboding steal over him.

Still, the knight didn't at first seem inclined to actually do anything. He looked very impressive, the massive bulk of him braced in his alcove at a battle-ready stance and his plume high and fierce, but for a few minutes he did nothing *but* stand there.

Akish said: "What happens now?" rather impatiently, but as he did so the knight moved.

His blood-red sabatons screeched against the marble tiles as he swivelled to face the marble block and raised his axe in a smooth clinking of metal against metal.

"A forfeit is paid!" said a voice from the depths of the knight's visor. It sounded rather metallic itself.

"What forfeit?" Akish demanded. "We haven't done anything!"

The knight didn't reply. It simply brought its axe down in a sweeping arc of scarlet upon the black chopping block. The sound of blade meeting marble rang almost painfully through the room, a note of high, perilous music; and the axe sprang back up.

"Ow!" said Kako, covering her ears.

The knight looked around him once while the sound of his blade still sang around the room, and began to disappear.

"Stop him!" shouted Akish.

Rafiq watched the knight disappear completely, and said: "How?"

"Blister it, how should I know, you son of a lizard! You've let him get away!"

"I don't think any of us could have stopped him," said Kako. "I'm not sure that I really *want* him here, if it comes to that."

Prince Akish made a frustrated noise and flung himself away

across the room. Kako met Rafiq's eyes, amusement mingling with caution, and gave her half shrug. A moment later, she said: "Is it just my ears, or is that clanging still going?"

"It's still going," said Prince Akish sourly. He had one hand against the far wall, his fingers tapping. "It's got into the walls."

"Into the walls? What do you mean?"

"They're ringing," the prince said. "Put your hand against one. You'll feel it."

Rafiq cautiously laid a palm on the wall closest to him, and the suggestion of sound in the air merged with the ringing in the wall. That was curious, but curiouser still was the fact that as he was pushing his palm against the wall, the wall seemed to be pushing back.

"Oh!" said Kako. She was just a little further down from him, and she was clutching her hand to her chest as though the wall had bitten her. "It moved! Rafiq–!"

"I felt it," he said grimly. As a matter of fact, the wall was still moving. Rafiq took a step back, straightened his arm, and laid the palm of it flat against the wall once again. Kako, who had come closer in curiosity, watched as his arm was forced into a bend and until the wall encroached almost to Rafiq's toes.

"How far by your count?" called Akish.

Rafiq met Kako's worried eyes. "Perhaps two and a half yards in total."

"I concur. This wall also moved by approximately two and a half yards. Did the others move?"

"The northern wall moved, but the southern didn't," said Kako. "The Keep obviously doesn't want to obstruct the Knight."

"Ominous," observed Akish. "We're at the top of the hour: I expect the pantomime will happen again at the next hour."

Kako, her eyes very wide and thoughtful, said: "That seems sensible. If the walls are moving at a rate of two and a half yards from every side, every hour, how long will it be before we're crushed?"

Akish paced the room swiftly, counting aloud, and at length met them at their wall on a count of one hundred yards.

"That gives us a little less than twenty hours to find a way out," said Kako. She blew her cheeks out and gazed around the room. "Nineteen, to be safe."

"There must be another way out," Prince Akish muttered. "Spread out! Find it! We'll come together again for the hour."

Rafiq, who had been puzzling over the room in the privacy of his own thoughts, said: "Why the knight?"

Kako's eyes flicked up at him and away.

Akish said: "What do you mean, lizard?"

"The walls are drawing in," Rafiq said slowly. "If we don't find our way out we'll be crushed."

Akish shifted impatiently. "As we observed. What of it?"

"Then why the knight?"

"Why anything in this accursed place?" said Akish, but he looked thoughtful. "However, if we're bound to die by one peril, why introduce a second?"

Rafiq gave a slight nod. It was the same question that had been exercising his mind.

"Turn your mind to finding a way out of this scrape," Prince Akish said. "I will think on the matter myself."

He was lucky, Rafiq thought with a slight, grim smile, that Akish hadn't spoken his remark as a Command. The prince hadn't yet been so dictatorial as to Command Rafiq's thoughts, and it would have been remarkably short-sighted to begin now, when the problem to be solved required as much thought as possible.

Rafiq thought he might already have something of an idea of what needed to be done to finish the seventh Circle. It wasn't an idea that appealed to him, however, and he was quite certain that it would have even less appeal for him when it occurred to Prince Akish. Far better not to openly speculate on it just yet: better to wait until they'd exhausted every other option before bringing out his theory.

Kako remained nearby, following quietly and unobtrusively in the background; not quite with him but not by herself, either. She didn't seem to be particularly concerned with trying to find a way out of the Circle: Rafiq saw her eyes flick most often away to where the red knight had appeared. Her spell-webbed hand, which had been in her pocket, was now flexing open and closed by her side as the spell grew.

Rafiq opened his mouth to ask: "What *is* that?" but by then Prince Akish was calling impatiently across the room at them.

"Wench! Put yourself to it! We have no time for your vagaries!"

Kako gave slight sniff of laughter, though her eyes remained solemn. It was the least sarcastic and the most serious Rafiq had ever seen her. Still, she seemed to turn her mind more thoroughly upon the problem of finding a way out, her spell apparently forgotten and unused in her hand.

She was diligently running her hands over the corner opposite the alcove when the prince said sharply: "Hark!" and the red knight winked into being. He went through the same routine as he had the first time; silence, the screeching of metal on tile as he turned, and then the metallic call of: "A forfeit has been paid!" before the ringing blade of the axe set the walls humming again.

Kako, who had already put her hands over her ears, said: "Hey!" in surprise. Rafiq and Prince Akish turned hastily to face her, and found that the walls had begun to move already. Not only had they begun to move sooner than the first time, they had begun to move *faster*: Kako was unexpectedly and unceremoniously being shoved further into the middle of the room. This time, moreover, the distance they moved was nearly four yards.

She said: "That throws our calculations out a bit, don't you think? What now?"

They shared a moment of speechlessness that was as complete

as it was hopeless. Then Rafiq said: "The Keep is trying to speed it along. Why hurry us?"

He hoped—oh *how* he hoped!—that Akish wasn't following the chain of events to its logical end. But Prince Akish, his eyes dark and hard, said: "The matter is perfectly clear. One of us will have to die for the others."

One of us not being Akish, Rafiq was certain. The thought sprang to his mind of the constructed story in the sixth Circle and he looked around again, hoping to see the sickening duality of sight that indicated the Keep had made copies of them all again. His sight remained horribly clear: they weren't dealing with constructs. It was the real Kako who could die, the real Akish who would Burden Rafiq either to put Kako's head or his own on the block, and the real Rafiq who would have to do or die.

Rafiq was still in the sick throes of processing his thoughts when Prince Akish hit Kako at the base of her skull with the hilt of his dagger. She gasped a little and crumpled where she stood, a pile of rather dirty, creased pink silk.

Akish said coldly: "There. You're Burdened. Place her on the block."

The Burden didn't fall. Rafiq, who had started grimly across the room with the determination of placing his own head on the block before the Burden could call him back to do what he couldn't bear to do, first doubted, then fiercely rejoiced. The Keep was interfering again. He couldn't turn dragon, either; which was unfortunate. But when he strode back across the room to Akish and Kako, the prince was so sure he was returning to do as he was Commanded that he didn't attempt to move. Secure in the safety of Rafiq's Thrall—the certainty that Rafiq couldn't harm him in any way—he didn't move when Rafiq stalked closer still. He only had time to look surprised when Rafiq tore his sword from its scabbard and thrust him through the throat.

Akish fell as swiftly but not as quietly as Kako, the gurgle of blood in his throat and lungs. The blade slid free of his throat as he dropped, and Rafiq let it fall beside him on the tiles, silently watching the blood spread. He would have preferred to kill Akish as a dragon; but whether by blade or tooth, the prince was dead and Kako would be safe. She would make it through the seventh Circle, and once beyond it there would be no Akish to menace either her or the princess.

It seemed to take a long time for the knight to appear again. Rafiq sank to his knees beside the chopping block at first, wanting to be ready for the blade when it appeared, but when moments stretched into minutes he settled back on his haunches. Eventually he sat on the block itself with a worried glance toward Kako, who could come around at any minute, and—if her past behaviour was any indicator—could only be depended upon to try and talk him out of it. That, he thought, suddenly chilled, or to try and take his place.

He spent his last few minutes wondering if he should tie Kako up; and then, having come to the decision that he *should*, in worrying that she wouldn't be able to untie herself when the seventh Circle ended and she regained consciousness. He was on the point of rising from the block to tie her up anyway, when the red knight materialised again in a horribly familiar clanking of armour. With a thin, cold sweat across his forehead and suddenly cold hands, Rafiq slipped sideways from the block until he was kneeling again. He heard the motion of the knight's upward stroke in deliberate, steady clanging of metal against metal, and laid his head on the block, his gaze on Kako. He was conscious of a desire that she would wake up, if only to be able to see her curious sideways smile again, but the desire was short-lived. He didn't want her last memory of him to be his head rolling across the marble floors.

The knight said in its grating metallic voice: "A forfeit is paid."

Rafiq closed his eyes briefly, but it seemed more pleasant to die with his eyes on Kako than with them closed, so he opened them again.

Metal shifted and whirred above his head, a bloody shadow shifting swiftly across the marble floor, and Rafiq's life thread was cut in a single, sharp stroke.

* * *

THREE FIGURES APPEARED in the seventh Circle. *A* seventh Circle. *One more* seventh Circle. The second seventh Circle, to be exact. As they had done in the first seventh Circle, Prince Akish, Rafiq, and Kako examined the circular chopping block. This time, however, Kako lingered behind the other two. It was evident that she could see the chopping block between the two men: it was likewise evident that she understood exactly what it was meant for, and between her fingers grew a small, potent, cobwebby piece of magic. It remained unused but undismissed while they explored to the edges of the room, and even when the red knight stalked from nothingness and into unpleasant reality she kept it still. It wasn't until they became aware of the creeping movement of the walls that it grew in intensity.

Rafiq's eyes flickered toward it once or twice, but he didn't remark on it until the knight had appeared for the second time, and the walls began to move more swiftly. Then he said at last: "What's that?"

Kako looked up at him with a bland face. "What?"

"Kako."

She smiled faintly. "You're really not very good at this game. For a man—dragon—who speaks as little as you do, you seem to have trouble getting right to the point."

"What is the spell you've been making?"

"I'll show you that in a bit," said Kako. She seemed to be breathing slightly faster now, a nervous in and out that drove the colour to her cheeks. "There's something more important that you should know."

Rafiq looked down at her curiously. "Another of your games?"

"Oh no. Deadly serious." Kako ran her free hand along the wall and then laid her ear against it. She continued: "I stole something from Akish a little while ago."

"I remember," said Rafiq. "You smuggled it to Dai and Zen."

"Yes. I had some ideas about it. It turns out that those ideas were correct."

"What was it?"

Kako shrugged her shoulder. "I'm still not exactly sure what it is. But I knew what it was being used for."

Rafiq, perhaps in an attempt to be as close to the point as possible, repeated her words back to her: "What was it being used for?"

"Your Thrall, mostly."

Rafiq's eyes fixed on her face, burning bright. "He was carrying the source of my Thrall *on* him? And you have it?"

"Yes."

"Give it to me!"

"It wouldn't do you any good," Kako said. She was certainly smiling now, though that smile had an edge of sadness to it.

Perhaps Rafiq caught the amusement, because he smiled in spite of his patent eagerness. "What do you mean by that?"

"Oh, well done!" said Kako. "A day or two ago you would have asked me 'Why?' and I could have spun that out for a very long time. What I mean by it is two things: one, that even if you had the source, you wouldn't be able to break it. It's specifically spelled against you. The second is that I've already unbound you from it. You've not been under Thrall these last few days."

"*Not* under Thrall! But I've felt– there was–" began Rafiq. He stopped, thoughts working visibly across his face, and at last he laughed, low and long. "I've been so long under Thrall that I've made a habit of it."

"You remember I said once that you were inured to the Thrall?"

"It was broken then?"

"The night before," nodded Kako. "It was simple enough to break because it wasn't what the original maker intended. Akish's father was very clever about it, but once I had a loose end it was as easy to unravel as a piece of knit. I only wonder that he used it for something like this when it has such potential."

"I'd like to see it."

"I thought you might," nodded Kako. She flicked a quick look at Akish, who was searching at the base of the chopping block, then passed Rafiq a small glinting thing with a sharp edge.

"It's part of a sword," he said quietly, turning it over. Again there was the play of swift and revelatory thought over his face. "I know something of a sword, a broken sword."

Kako's eyes snapped to his face, and she laughed once, oddly. "Of *course* you do! When this Circle is done, you'll have to tell Dai. She's got some ideas about it as well: she thinks it might be capable of keeping the Fae from invading."

"I thought you were the one trying to keep the Fae from Shinpo."

"Well, I am," said Kako, looking vaguely uncomfortable. "But so is Dai, and she's already experimented with the shard. I suppose there *are* more pieces to it?"

Rafiq nodded. "At least five. When pieced together it's supposed to become a powerful talisman."

"Do you know what sort of talisman?"

"Something about binding and protection. I suppose that's why Akish's father was able to use it on me."

"I suppose," agreed Kako. She sent a brief, covert look over her shoulder to the alcove that would soon hold the red knight. Then she said to Rafiq: "I suppose we shouldn't talk about it when Akish could overhear. What were we talking about before the sword?"

"You said you'd show me the spell you've been working since we discovered the alcove."

"So I did," said Kako. "All right. It's really a very simple one."

"What does it do?"

Kako held out the spell, stretched now between the fingers of both hands. "It's easier if I show you," she said, in a voice so light, so reasonable. And Rafiq, who still hadn't mastered all the games, leaned closer.

The webbing of spell caught him fairly in the face, spreading rapidly over his features until it knit at the back of his head. Rafiq swayed, began to speak, and fell. He was unconscious before he hit the tiles.

Prince Akish, who was watching from the other side of the room, said: "A clever little piece of work. I was going to hit you over the head in any case, wench."

Kako gave a particularly elegant shrug. "I doubt it would have done you any good. I've got the distinct feeling that it has to be a personal sacrifice. If you'd slaughtered me I think you'd only have found the walls moving a little more quickly. Then one of you would have had to sacrifice yourselves anyway."

"I wouldn't have slaughtered you," said Akish loftily. "Rafiq would have done it. And I rather fancy that it *would* have been a sacrifice."

"You can't sacrifice what doesn't belong to you," said Kako. "I'm the only one who can sacrifice me."

"It's nearly the top of the hour," Prince Akish said. His eyes were bright and excited.

Kako looked at him meditatively. "I don't really want to talk to you any more," she said. "Perhaps you could be kind enough to shut up now."

Prince Akish's jaw dropped open. "How dare you, you misbegotten wench!"

"I'm not, actually," said Kako. She settled herself beside the chopping block quite calmly, but from the way she quickly dashed the palms of her hands against her silk trousers, it was clear she had begun to sweat. "Misbegotten, I mean. Oh, and I'd be very careful when you get through the seventh Circle, if I were you."

The red knight was appearing, sharp, metallic and menacing.

Jeeringly, the prince said: "Indeed? And why is that?"

Kako looked up at the knight once, and then away again. She removed her neck scarf with an almost ceremonial solemnity, then stooped to lay her head on the block, warm flesh meeting cold marble.

"I broke your Thrall on him," she said. "It won't be long before he realises it."

"A forfeit is paid," said the knight. The axe rose, dripping with bloody shadows.

Kako said: "If I were you, I would want to be *very* far away from him when he discovers that fact."

Akish's face froze in a mask of fear, fury, and eye-bulging incredulity. "You misbegotten daughter of a pig! What have you done?"

Kako laughed, and the blade laughed with her. Then there was only ringing silence.

The Seventh Circle is ended.

9

THE CIRCLES OPENED

There was a fraction of a moment when Rafiq was certain he was dead. He felt the cold slice of steel across the side of his neck and through his throat, and there was an instant of absolute extinguishment. Then he found himself alive and whole, kneeling on cold, hard tile with one hand supporting him. He was shaking, left with the horrible certainty that he had indeed died and was yet still alive.

At length Rafiq rose carefully and stood upright on the blood-red tiles. Where was Kako? She should have made it through the seventh Circle as well, unless– had the Keep been playing its tricks again? The air—no, space and time—seemed to split, and then Kako was there, too. She was kneeling as he had been, her face almost powder-white, and as he stepped forward swiftly she raised her head, shivering. Her scarf had been removed, baring her neck: it was clenched in her left hand, the fingers white about it.

Rafiq dropped to one knee beside her and pulled her close, acting on another of those human instincts that were taking him by surprise so much lately. When Kako ceased to shake he took her scarf and draped it around her neck again, pinning it to her head-dress with more goodwill than skill.

By way of taking her mind off the death she'd encountered and overcome, he said: "Where's Akish?"

"I don't think he'll be coming through," she said.

Rafiq's heart sank. If Akish was dead, Rafiq's Burden would pass back to the Crown and he would soon be forced to fly back to Illisr under duress.

"You think he's dead?"

"I'm sure of it," said Kako. A moment later, Rafiq was sure of it too.

At first the yells were angry ones: and it was certainly Prince Akish's voice. Then they became shouts of fear. Within moments the prince was screaming as the Keep rumbled beneath their feet. Kako had her hands pressed to her ears, the tears gliding down her unnaturally white cheeks, but Rafiq listened until the screams died away. It didn't take long. There was no pleasure in it, but he wanted to be sure that Akish really was dead, that he wouldn't suddenly appear next to Kako.

When the screams stopped, Kako took her hands away from her ears and wiped away her tears. "I told him he shouldn't enter the seventh Circle," she said quietly, without quite meeting Rafiq's eyes. "I *told* him."

"The Burden," Rafiq said, his voice slightly hoarse. He couldn't help remembering those moving walls, and he wasn't sure that Prince Akish's screams had really faded from the stones of the Keep. "It should be bearing down on me, pulling me back to Illisr."

Much to his relief, his remark had the effect of taking the sick look away from Kako's eyes. "Oh, that's interesting," she said. "I already had this conversation with you. Well, with a version of you, I suppose. The Burden won't bother you again. Actually, you haven't been really Burdened since the third Circle, when I picked

Prince Akish's pockets. He had a shard of sword in a hidden pocket; I felt it the moment he entered the Keep, but it wasn't until I investigated a bit that I realised he was using it to control you."

"Since the *third* Circle? Why didn't you tell me?"

"I thought it would be best to let you get used to it slowly," she said. "You've been Burdened for a long time. I didn't want you to feel overwhelmed."

There was a little part of Rafiq's mind that suggested this answered the question of why he had been able to do certain things that he shouldn't have been able to do. There were several times when he had obeyed Prince Akish sheerly out of habit, when the—shard, was it?—had been out of the prince's possession.

Kako was still looking a little bit crushed and pale when he finally opened his mouth to speak, so instead of saying any of the frustrated, furious things that he wanted to say to her, Rafiq merely said: "You said it was a shard of sword the Burden was held in. Show me."

"It wasn't exactly *held* in there," Kako said, reaching into one all-but-invisible pocket in her pink silk trousers. "It's more that the sword piece has a specific kind of enchantment laid upon it, and the king was able to twist it a bit to make your Thrall. I untwisted it."

She passed him the small piece of metal carefully; almost reverently. Rafiq took it just as carefully, and hissed between his teeth. "It's part of a Faery blade!"

"Yes," she said. "But the enchantment on it– it's not Fae."

"No," said Rafiq. "It's not. I've heard stories of a blade once whole and then broken."

"What stories?" demanded Kako. "I think this piece of sword can help us get rid of the fae who've migrated here."

Rafiq turned it in his fingers, a smile playing on his lips. It was almost tangibly delicious to know something that Kako, pert little thing that she was, didn't know. "I'm certain it can," he said.

He slipped the shard into his own pocket, ignoring Kako's wrathful look, and added: "Since we're here, we may as well rescue the princess."

"She doesn't need rescuing," Kako said, her cheeks dusky with annoyance. "She came here specifically to get away from that kind of thing. She's been trying to find a way to get rid of the Fae and close the doors to Faery, and she couldn't do that while suitors were calling."

"She ran away from *suitors*?"

"There were a lot of them! And they would keep calling in the mornings, when she was trying to work on her theories and searching through the library. She couldn't even travel to visit libraries in other countries without people thinking that a match between Shinpo and them would be a rather good idea."

"Beautiful, is she?" asked Rafiq, really looking around the room for the first time. It was a surprisingly small one, tiled with the same red tiles that Rafiq had come to expect of the Keep proper, but here the walls and the ceiling were also the same shade of vermillion. The effect, after the seventh Circle, was reminiscent of blood covering and subsuming the whole room.

"Not really," muttered Kako. "But Shinpo has a lot of nobles, and it's a good match for any of their young men. Not to mention that she's third to the throne, so the surrounding kingdoms don't find it a bad match, either. And then there are princes like Akish, who think it's useful to have a Shinpoan princess in their power."

"We've come all this way," said Rafiq, unwilling to be swayed. The princess would be the one possible obstacle to his staying at the Keep, and he would rather have that obstacle out of the way as quickly as possible.

"I'd like to see her. You said she's usually under enchanted sleep anyway, didn't you?"

"Not exactly," said Kako, moving with him as he walked toward the only door in the room. She was tugging on his arm ineffectively; almost amusingly. *"Rafiq!"*

But he had already opened the door, impelled by his sense of curiosity as much as by his sense of mischief. He found himself in a large suite, its gently curving walls formed from the tower's outer walls: this, then was the highest room of the tower. There were two heavily veiled sections—the powder-room and the bathing-room, Rafiq guessed—and one large canopied bed that should have been occupied.

It wasn't. And as he stepped further into the suite, his eyes sweeping over the room, the cobwebby disuse of it began to sink in. As magnificent as everything was, it was a decayed magnificence. There was deep, oily dust on all the furniture: it hadn't been dusted in months, perhaps years. The rich veiling, seen closer to, proved to be full of moths and trailing threads. With each step that Rafiq took he made a footprint on the mildewy tiles and rugs alike.

"It's not a very comfortable room," said Kako, with a sigh. When it became evident that she couldn't stop him, she'd ceased to try, and had sat down glumly on a dusty wooden chair instead. "The wind shakes it so loudly that you can't sleep, and the fire either roars so high it's abominably hot, or dies away and leaves you to freeze. Besides, some of the challengers were bright enough to try to scale the tower from the outside. It wasn't safe."

Rafiq only half heard her. He was remembering something Kako had said many days ago. She had said that the princess was kept under enchanted sleep while the dragon was out of the Keep. Akish had assumed that this was because the dragon didn't want her to escape, and Rafiq, who didn't at that stage know that Kako was herself the dragon, had found it a reasonable assumption. Now, however, he *did* know it. His eyes dwelt thoughtfully and a little amusedly on Kako, who was looking at the floor. What was it that Zen had said, later on? Kako had immediately silenced him, but during the game in the fourth Circle she had admitted that when she turned dragon, she kept her human form.

That form, she had said, remained in a deep sleep while her consciousness inhabited the form of a dragon.

The princess slept while the dragon was active because *the princess was the dragon.*

Rafiq, slightly stunned, said: "*You're* the princess! You're the *princess!*"

"Oh, well done!" Kako said, irritably sarcastic.

"But I met your mother! Your sisters and your brother!"

"Yes. Queen Shiori of Shinpo to almost everyone else. Oh, and Crown Princess Akira, second Princess Suki, Princess Dai, Prince Zen and little Princess Mee. I think the only one you didn't meet was my father. He's the king-consort, in case it wasn't obvious to you."

"Then why did you–" Rafiq stopped the bewildered thought where it started, and began to laugh. It was obvious why she had pretended to be the princess' maid. How else could she fend off would-be suitors? Much easier to go along with the men that made it past the first Circle, and sabotage them where she could.

"Exactly," said Kako. She was watching him again. "I'd appreciate it if you don't spread it about."

"Who would I spread it to? Does the Keep get so many visitors?"

"No, barely any. Wait, what do you mean by that?"

"I like it here," said Rafiq. "And as a dragon I'm faster, stronger, and deadlier than you."

"Well, there's no need to be smug about–"

"I want to stay here."

"Why didn't you say so right away?" Kako demanded. She sounded slightly miffed. "There are dozens of free rooms, and I'm sure if you're polite enough about it the Keep will arrange a dragon-sized one for you with access to the open air."

Rafiq, his heart glad, said: "You don't mind?"

"Mind? Why should I? You're pretty easy to live with, after all. Besides I want to know about the sword."

"I see." Rafiq, struggling between disappointment and amusement, said: "I'm to be useful to you."

"Oh, well, I've gotten used to you already," said Kako, shrugging. "I'd rather have you here than anyone else."

All things considered, thought Rafiq, his smile a little less rueful, that wasn't so bad of a place to start. "Where do you live in this bewildering old heap?"

"Usually downstairs," Kako said, springing lightly from her chair. She was significantly more cheerful than she had been earlier. "Though when there are no challengers I keep the passage open between here and home–"

"The palace."

"–yes, the palace. Then we can come and go as we please. I always sleep here, though."

Rafiq, thinking of tiny Miyoko walking the halls alone, said: "You let that little scrap wander the halls here?"

"Oh yes, the Keep loves her! Almost as much as it loves me, as a matter of fact."

"Me, on the other hand," said Dai's voice from the doorway; "It positively loathes!"

"You shouldn't have tried to force it to make new rooms in winter, then," said Kako. "What are you doing here?"

"Just making sure you're not dead," said Dai, smiling somewhat maliciously. "We all are."

"*All?*"

"We're all here," said Zen, ducking beneath her arm. "Even Father is here. You're in a lot of trouble, young lady."

"But–"

"Akira isn't here," Dai contradicted. "She's still in a state meeting."

Zen, with a likewise gleeful malice, added: "A state meeting that Mother ran away from when the passage disappeared, by the way."

"*By* the way," echoed Miyoko, kicking at Dai's legs to make room for herself.

"It disappeared?" Kako's eyes found Rafiq's: she looked surprised and very slightly uneasy. "It shouldn't have done that!"

"That's what we thought," said a familiar voice from the door. Dai immediately vacated the doorway, as did the other two, and Rafiq was left to wonder how he could ever have thought that Kako's mother was a servant. She was entirely regal. Even if she hadn't been wearing the royal seal in her head-dress, she would have been obvious as royalty today.

"My dear little clever one, you *could* have found it in your heart to come over and tell us you were safe," she said. She said it in a kindly—even a gentle—voice, but Kako went pink.

"I'm sorry," she said. "I didn't know the seventh Circle would make the passage disappear."

"What happened?" asked a deeper male voice.

Kako's father, Rafiq thought. The man's eyes were on him, thoughtful and faintly challenging. If those eyes didn't have ingrained lines of good humoured amusement beside them, Rafiq might even have thought them hard. Nor was he native-born Shinpoan—so *that* was where Zen had inherited his eyes—though he spoke Shinpoan like a native.

Kako, who hadn't noticed anything amiss, said: "We entered the seventh Circle. I've got an idea that the Keep did something very big while we were in there, because it wasn't Constructs and copies of ourselves this time."

"I died," said Rafiq. He was becoming rapidly more certain that it was the truth.

"Me too," Kako said, her mouth quirking in an involuntary grimace. "I think the Keep might have created several alternate timelines. That would take enough of its power to drain all the non-essential magics around the place."

"We should be able to prove or disprove that," said Kako's father. He had forgotten Rafiq in his interest. "It's far more likely that it's a simple case of timeline manipulation, though. What other non-essentials were drained?"

"I haven't checked yet," said Kako. "And it *can't* be manipulation, because–"

"Don't let them start talking, Mother!" said Suki in despair. "They'll never stop!"

Rafiq found himself grinning. Nobody seemed to pay any attention to Suki's plea: Kako and her father continued to argue back and forth about the relative merits of timeline manipulation and alternate timelines. Dai and Zen, who were both listening intently, occasionally interposed a question or comment. To Rafiq, it sounded like the same thing with a different name.

Queen Shiori, who must have been used to the babble of almost incomprehensible debate in the background of her days, smiled at Rafiq and said: "I'm glad you came through safely, my dear."

Why was it, wondered Rafiq, that the queen always made him feel like a fledgling before its tutor? Not quite grown up and slightly gawky. He said: "So am I, your majesty."

"I've been drawing up citizenship papers for you. Do you still intend to remain here?"

"Yes, your majesty."

"Well, we might have to go away for a little bit in a year or two," said Kako, suddenly attentive. "Rafiq knows something about a magical artefact that might be very useful in chasing out the Fae. I just need to do some experiments on the bit I have, first."

"We'll talk about that in a year or two," said Queen Shiori, her eyes flicking from Kako to Rafiq. "Now that I'm assured you're safe, my little clever one, I think I really must return to my meeting. My darling, will you walk with me?"

She was addressing her husband, asking a question that Rafiq knew very well wasn't the one spoken. He saw the brief passage of silent communication that passed between the two of them, and then Kako's father nodded. "How could I resist?" he said. There was a smile in his voice, but it was less pronounced when he said to Rafiq in passing: "We'll talk later, I think."

Rafiq nodded silently, very aware of the curious eyes of Dai, Zen, and above all, Kako.

"And Mee has lessons," said Suki firmly. "So does Zen."

Zen grumbled beneath his breath, but allowed himself to be shooed away to the door. "Wait for me before you start working on the shard," he said beseechingly.

Dai, catching the pointed look that Suki sent her, said: "Don't even think about it, Suki! My tutor doesn't want to see me again until he's had a chance to see if he can prove me wrong about time-release mechanics in preservative spells."

Suki cast a look of weary long-suffering up at the ceiling and towed Zen and Miyoko away.

Dai collapsed languidly into one of the chairs and said: "Ugh! What a nasty little room this is."

"I know," said Kako, not at all offended. "Why do you think I don't live here?"

"Well, why not fit it out for Rafiq? Open out a few of the windows and turn the dressing room into a flight-run?"

"Now *there's* a thought," Kako said. To Rafiq, she said: "So Mother has been drawing up papers of citizenship for you! She seems quite pleased that you'll be here with me, actually."

"Well, you're a sort-of dragon and he's a sort-of human," said Dai, shrugging. "It's a good match."

"Match?" Kako looked startled and a little confused.

Rafiq's eyes sought Dai's in silent pleading. She was looking sarcastic and more than slightly malicious, but after a moment her eyes dropped. She said: "Well, if you *have* to have someone in the Keep with you, he's a good choice. He'll be able to keep up with you, at any rate."

Kako laughed suddenly. "Oh, there's no doubt about that!

What do you think, Rafiq? Do you think you'd like to live up here?"

Up or down didn't matter, of course. So long as the Keep housed Kako, Rafiq would make his bed in the smallest and dankest of its rooms. But this room at the top of the tower– this room had enough space for a much larger dragon than Rafiq. Or perhaps, in time, two dragons.

"This will be just right," he said.